George MacDonald

GEORGE MacDONALD, Scottish novelist, poet, and clergy-man, was born on his family's farm in Aberdeenshire in 1824. After completing his education at King's College, he went to London as a tutor. There he met Louisa Powell, with whom he had a long and happy marriage and eleven children.

MacDonald was ordained a Congregationalist minister but resigned because his parishioners complained about his free-thinking sermons. His claim to immortality rests on his allegori-cal fairy stories, tales he told to his children, which first appeared in the 1870s in the magazine *Good Words for the Young*. Such enchanting classics as *At the Back of the North Wind*, *The Princess and the Goblin* and its sequel, *The Princess and Curdie*, *The Golden Key*, and *The Light Princess* stand out for their dreamlike, spiritual quality.

George MacDonald's many admirers included Tennyson, Mark Twain, and Emerson. Lewis Carroll showed the first version of *Alice's Adventures in Wonderland* to the MacDonald family to see if they thought it worth publishing. And the goblins in J.R.R. Tolkien's famed *The Hobbit* and *The Lord of the Rings* are much like those in *The Princess and the Goblin*, a childhood favorite of Tolkien's.

MacDonald died in England in 1905. The poet W. H. Auden once said that MacDonald's ". . . most extraordinary, and pre-cious, gift is his ability, in all his stories, to create an atmo-sphere of goodness about which there is nothing phony or moralistic. Nothing is rarer in literature."

Works of lasting literary merit by classic international writers

YEARLING BOOKS/YOUNG YEARLINGS/YEARLING CLASSICS are designed especially to entertain and enlighten young people. Patricia Reilly Giff, consultant to this series, received her bachelor's degree from Marymount College and a master's degree in history from St. John's University. She holds a Professional Diploma in Reading and a Doctorate of Humane Letters from Hofstra University. She was a teacher and reading consultant for many years, and is the author of numerous books for young readers.

For a complete listing of all Yearling titles,
write to Dell Readers Service,
P.O. Box 1045, South Holland, IL 60473.

The Princess and the Goblin

George MacDonald

With an Afterword by Andre Norton

Published by
Dell Publishing
a division of
Bantam Doubleday Dell Publishing Group, Inc.
666 Fifth Avenue
New York, New York 10103

ISBN: 0-440-47189-3

RL: 5.5

Printed in the United States of America

August 1990

12 11 10 9 8 7 6 5 4

OPM

Contents

The Princess
and the Goblin

Chapter 1

Why the Princess Has a Story About Her

*T*HERE was once a little princess whose father was king over a great country full of mountains and valleys. His palace was built upon one of the mountains, and was very grand and beautiful. The princess, whose name was Irene, was born there, but she was sent soon after her birth, because her mother was not very strong, to be brought up by country people in a large house, half castle, half farmhouse, on the side of another mountain, about halfway between its base and its peak.

The princess was a sweet little creature, and at the time my story begins was about eight years old, I think, but she got older very fast. Her face was fair and pretty, with eyes like two bits of night sky, each with a star dissolved in the blue. Those eyes you would have thought must have known they came from there, so often were they turned up in that direction. The ceiling of her nursery was blue, with stars in it, as like the sky as they could make it. But I doubt if ever she saw the real sky with the stars in it, for a reason which I had better mention at once.

These mountains were full of hollow places underneath: huge caverns, and winding ways, some with water running through them, and some shining with all colors of the rainbow when a light was taken in. There would not have been much known about them, had there not been mines there, great deep pits, with long galleries and passages running off from them, which had been dug to get at the ore of which the mountains were full. In the course of digging, the miners came upon many of these natural caverns. A few of them had far-off openings out on the side of a mountain, or into a ravine.

Now in these subterranean caverns lived a strange race of beings, called by some gnomes, by some kobolds, by some goblins. There was a legend current in the country that at one time they lived aboveground, and were very like other people. But for some reason or other, concerning which there were different legendary theories, the king had laid what they thought too severe taxes upon them, or had required observances of them they did not like, or had begun to treat them with more severity, in some way or other, and impose stricter laws; and the consequence was that they had all disappeared from the face of the country.

According to the legend, however, instead of going to some other country, they had all taken refuge in the subterranean caverns, whence they never came out but at night, and then seldom showed themselves in any numbers, and never to many people at once. It was only in the least frequented and most difficult parts of the mountains that they were said to gather even at night in the open air. Those who had caught sight of any of them said that they had greatly altered in the course of generations; and no wonder, seeing they lived away from the sun, in cold and wet and dark places. They were now not ordinarily ugly but either absolutely hideous, or ludicrously grotesque in face and form. There was no invention, they said, of the most lawless imagination expressed by pen or pencil, that could surpass the extravagance of their appearance. But I suspect those who said so had mistaken some of their animal companions for the goblins themselves—of which more by and by. The goblins themselves were not so far removed from the human as such a description would imply. And as they grew misshapen in body they had grown in knowledge and cleverness, and now were able to do things no mortal could see the possibility of. But as they grew in cunning, they grew in mischief, and their great delight was in every way they could think of to annoy the people who lived in the open-air story above them.

They had enough of affection left for each other to preserve them from being absolutely cruel for cruelty's sake to those that came in their way, but still they so heartily cherished the ancestral grudge against those who occupied their former possessions, and especially against the descendants of the king who had caused their expulsion, that they sought every opportunity of tormenting them in ways that were as odd as their inventors; and although dwarfed and misshapen, they had strength equal to their cunning. In the process of time they had got a king and a government of their own, whose chief business, beyond their own simple affairs, was to devise trouble for their neighbors. It will now be pretty evident why the little princess had never seen the sky at night. They were much too afraid of the goblins to let her out of the house then, even in company with ever so many attendants; and they had good reason, as we shall see by and by.

Chapter 2

The Princess Loses Herself

I HAVE said the Princess Irene was about eight years old when my story begins. And this is how it begins.

One very wet day, when the mountain was covered with mist which was constantly gathering itself together into raindrops, and pouring down on the roofs of the great old house, whence it fell in a fringe of water from the eaves all round about it, the princess could not of course go out. She got very tired, so tired that even her toys could no longer amuse her. You would wonder at that if I had time to describe to you one half of the toys she had. But then, you wouldn't have the toys themselves, and that makes all the difference: you can't get tired of a thing before you have it. It was a picture, though, worth seeing—the princess sitting in the nursery with the sky ceiling over her head, at a great table covered with her toys. If the artist would like to draw this, I should advise him not to meddle with the toys. I am afraid of attempting to describe them, and I think he had better not try to draw them. He had better not. He can do a thousand things I can't, but I don't think he could draw those toys. No man could better make the princess herself than he could, though—leaning with her back bowed into the back of the chair, her head hanging down, and her hands in her lap, very miserable, as she would say herself, not even knowing what she would like, except it were to go out and get thoroughly wet, and catch a particularly nice cold, and have to go to bed and take gruel. The next moment after you see her sitting there, her nurse goes out of the room.

Even that is a change, and the princess wakes up a little, and looks about her. Then she tumbles off her chair, and runs out of the door, not the same door the nurse went out of, but one which opened at the foot of a curious old stair of worm-eaten oak, which looked as if never anyone had set foot upon it. She had once before been up six steps, and that was sufficient reason, in such a day, for trying to find out what was at the top of it.

Up and up she ran—such a long way it seemed to her!—until she came to the top of the third flight. There she found the landing was the end of a long passage. Into this she ran. It was full of doors on each side. There were so many that she did not care to open any but ran on to the end, where she turned into another passage, also full of doors. When she had turned twice more, and still saw doors and only doors about her, she began to get frightened. It was so silent! And all those doors must hide rooms with nobody in them! That was dreadful. Also the rain made a great trampling noise on the roof. She turned and started at full speed, her little footsteps echoing through the sounds of the rain—back for the stairs and her safe nursery. So she thought, but she had lost herself long ago. It doesn't follow that she *was* lost, though, because she had lost herself.

She ran for some distance, turned several times, and then

began to be afraid. Very soon she was sure that she had lost the way back. Rooms everywhere, and no stair! Her little heart beat as fast as her little feet ran, and a lump of tears was growing in her throat. But she was too eager and perhaps too frightened to cry for some time. At last her hope failed her. Nothing but passages and doors everywhere! She threw herself on the floor, and burst into a wailing cry broken by sobs.

She did not cry long, however, for she was as brave as could be expected of a princess of her age. After a good cry, she got up and brushed the dust from her frock. Oh, what old dust it was! Then she wiped her eyes with her hands, for princesses don't always have their handkerchiefs in their pockets, any more than some other little girls I know of. Next, like a true princess, she resolved on going wisely to work to find her way back: she would walk through the passages, and look in every direction for the stair. This she did, but without success. She went over the same ground again and again without knowing it, for the passages and doors were all alike. At last, in a corner, through a half-open door, she did see a stair. But, alas, it went the wrong way: instead of going down, it went up. Frightened as she was, however, she could not help wishing to see where yet farther the stair could lead. It was very narrow, and so steep that she went on like a four-legged creature on her hands and feet.

Chapter 3

The Princess and—We Shall See Who

WHEN she came to the top, she found herself in a little square place, with three doors, two opposite each other, and one opposite the top of the stair. She stood for a moment, without an idea in her little head what to do next. But as she stood she began to hear a curious humming sound. Could it be the rain? No. It was much more gentle and even monotonous than the sound of the rain, which now she scarcely heard. The low sweet humming sound went on, sometimes stopping for a little while and then beginning again. It was more like the hum of a very happy bee that had found a rich well of honey in some globular flower, than anything else I can think of at this moment. Where could it come from? She laid her ear first to one of the doors to hearken if it was there—then to another. When she laid her ear against the third door, there could be no doubt where it came from: it must be from something in that room. What could it be? She was rather afraid, but her curiosity was stronger than her fear, and she opened the door very gently and peeped in. What do you think she saw? A very old lady who sat spinning.

Perhaps you will wonder how the princess could tell that the old lady was an old lady, when I inform you that not only was she beautiful, but her skin was smooth and white. I will tell you more. Her hair was combed back from her forehead and face, and hung loose far down and all over her back. That is not much like an old lady—is it? Ah, but it was white almost as snow! And although her face was so smooth, her eyes looked so wise that you could not have helped seeing she must be old. The princess, though she could not have told you why, did think her very old indeed—quite fifty, she said to herself. But she was rather older than that, as you shall hear.

While the princess stared bewildered, with her head just inside the door, the old lady lifted hers, and said, in a sweet, but old and rather shaky voice, which mingled very pleasantly with the continued hum of her wheel, "Come in, my dear, come in. I am glad to see you."

That the princess was a real princess you might see now quite plainly, for she didn't hang on to the handle of the door and stare without moving, as I have known some do who ought to have been princesses but were only rather vulgar little girls. She did as she was told, stepped inside the door at once, and shut it gently behind her.

"Come to me, my dear," said the old lady.

And again the princess did as she was told. She approached the old lady—rather slowly, I confess—but did not stop until she stood by her side, and looked up in her face with her blue eyes and the two melted stars in them.

"Why, what have you been doing with your eyes, child?" asked the old lady.

"Crying," answered the princess.

"Why, child?"

"Because I couldn't find my way down again."

"But you could find your way up."

"Not at first—not for a long time."

"But your face is streaked like the back of a zebra. Hadn't you a handkerchief to wipe your eyes with?"

"No."

"Then why didn't you come to me to wipe them for you?"

"Please, I didn't know you were here. I will next time."

"There's a good child!" said the old lady.

Then she stopped her wheel, and rose, and going out of the room, returned with a little silver basin and a soft white towel, with which she washed and wiped the bright little face. And the princess thought her hands were so smooth and nice!

When she carried away the basin and towel, the little princess wondered to see how straight and tall she was, for, although she was so old, she didn't stoop a bit. She was dressed in black velvet with thick white heavy-looking lace about it; and on the black dress her hair shone like silver. There was hardly any more furniture in the room than there might have been in that of the poorest old woman who made her bread by her spinning. There was no carpet on the floor—no table anywhere—nothing but the spinning wheel and the chair beside it. When she came back, she sat down again, and without a word began her spinning once more, while Irene, who had never seen a spinning wheel, stood by her side and looked on.

When the old lady had got her thread fairly going again, she said to the princess, but without looking at her, "Do you know my name, child?"

"No, I don't know it," answered the princess.

"My name is Irene."

"That's *my* name!" cried the princess.

"I know that. I let you have mine. I haven't got your name. You've got mine."

"How can that be?" asked the princess, bewildered. "I've always had my name."

"Your papa, the king, asked me if I had any objection to your having it; and, of course, I hadn't. I let you have it with pleasure."

"It was very kind of you to give me your name—and such a pretty one," said the princess.

"Oh, not so *very* kind!" said the old lady. "A name is one of those things one can give away and keep all the same. I have a good many such things. Wouldn't you like to know who I am, child?"

"Yes, that I should—very much."

"I'm your great-great-grandmother," said the lady.

"What's that?" asked the princess.

"I'm your father's mother's father's mother."

"Oh, dear! I can't understand that," said the princess.

"I daresay not. I didn't expect you would. But that's no reason why I shouldn't say it."

"Oh, no!" answered the princess.

"I will explain it all to you when you are older," the lady went on. "But you will be able to understand this much now: I came here to take care of you."

"Is it long since you came? Was it yesterday? Or was it today, because it was so wet that I couldn't get out?"

"I've been here ever since you came yourself."

"What a long time!" said the princess. "I don't remember it at all."

"No. I suppose not."

"But I never saw you before."

"No. But you shall see me again."

"Do you live in this room always?"

"I don't sleep in it. I sleep on the opposite side of the landing. I sit here most of the day."

"I shouldn't like it. My nursery is much prettier. You must be a queen too, if you are my great big grandmother."

"Yes, I am a queen."

"Where is your crown, then?"

"In my bedroom."

"I *should* like to see it."

"You shall someday—not today."

"I wonder why nursie never told me."

"Nursie doesn't know. She never saw me."

"But somebody knows that you are in the house?"

"No, nobody."

"How do you get your dinner, then?"

"I keep poultry—of a sort."

"Where do you keep them?"

"I will show you."

"And who makes the chicken broth for you?"

"I never kill any of my chickens."

"Then I can't understand."

"What did you have for breakfast this morning?" asked the lady.

"Oh! I had bread and milk, and an egg—I daresay you eat their eggs."

"Yes, that's it. I eat their eggs."

"Is that what makes your hair so white?"

"No, my dear. It's old age. I am very old."

"I thought so. Are you fifty?"

"Yes—more than that."

"Are you a hundred?"

"Yes—more than that. I am too old for you to guess. Come and see my chickens."

Again she stopped her spinning. She rose, took the princess by the hand, led her out of the room, and opened the door opposite the stair. The princess expected to see a lot of hens and chickens, but instead of that, she saw the blue sky first, and then the roofs of the house, with a multitude of the loveliest pigeons, mostly white, but of all colors, walking about, making bows to each other, and talking a language she could not understand. She clapped her hands with delight, and up rose such a flapping of wings that she in her turn was startled.

"You've frightened my poultry," said the old lady, smiling.

"And they've frightened me," said the princess, smiling too. "But what very nice poultry! Are the eggs nice?"

"Yes, very nice."

"What a small egg-spoon you must have! Wouldn't it be better to keep hens, and get bigger eggs?"

"How should I feed them, though?"

"I see," said the princess. "The pigeons feed themselves. They've got wings."

"Just so. If they couldn't fly, I couldn't eat their eggs."

"But how do you get at the eggs? Where are their nests?"

The lady took hold of a little loop of string in the wall at the side of the door and, lifting a shutter, showed a great many pigeonholes with nests, some with young ones and some with eggs in them. The birds came in at the other side, and she took out the eggs on this side. She closed it again quickly, lest the young ones should be frightened.

"Oh, what a nice way!" cried the princess. "Will you give me an egg to eat? I'm rather hungry."

"I will someday, but now you must go back, or nursie will be miserable about you. I daresay she's looking for you everywhere."

"Except here," answered the princess. "Oh, how surprised she *will* be when I tell her about my great big grand-grandmother!"

"Yes, that she will!" said the old lady with a curious smile. "Mind you tell her all about it exactly."

"That I will. Please will you take me back to her?"

"I can't go all the way, but I will take you to the top of the stair, and then you must run down quite fast into your own room."

The little princess put her hand in the old lady's, who, looking this way and that, brought her to the top of the first stair, and thence to the bottom of the second, and did not leave her till she saw her halfway down the third. When she heard the cry of her nurse's pleasure at finding her, she turned and walked up the stairs again, very fast indeed for such a very great grandmother, and sat down to her spinning with another strange smile on her sweet old face.

About this spinning of hers I will tell you more another time. Guess what she was spinning.

Chapter 4

What the Nurse Thought of It

"WHY, where can you have been, princess?" asked the nurse, taking her in her arms. "It's very unkind of you to hide away so long. I began to be afraid—"

Here she checked herself.

"What were you afraid of, nursie?" asked the princess.

"Never mind," she answered. "Perhaps I will tell you another day. Now tell me where you have been."

"I've been up a long way to see my very great, huge old grandmother," said the princess.

"What do you mean by that?" asked the nurse, who thought she was making fun.

"I mean that I've been a long way up and up to see my *great*-grandmother. Ah, nursie, you don't know what a beautiful mother of grandmothers I've got upstairs. She is *such* an old lady, with such lovely white hair—as white as my silver cup! Now, when I think of it, I think her hair must be silver."

"What nonsense you are talking, princess!" said the nurse.

"I'm not talking nonsense," returned Irene, rather offended. "I will tell you all about her. She's much taller than you, and much prettier."

"Oh, I daresay!" remarked the nurse.

"And she lives on pigeons' eggs."

"Most likely," said the nurse.

"And she sits in an empty room, spin-spinning all day long."

"Not a doubt of it," said the nurse.

"And she keeps her crown in her bedroom."

"Of course—quite the proper place to keep her crown in. She wears it in bed, I'll be bound."

"She didn't say that. And I don't think she does. That wouldn't be comfortable—would it? I don't think my papa wears his crown for a night-cap. Does he, nursie?"

"I never asked him. I daresay he does."

"And she's been there ever since I came here—ever so many years."

"Anybody could have told you that," said the nurse, who did not believe a word Irene was saying.

"Why didn't you tell me, then?"

"There was no necessity. You could make it all up for yourself."

"You don't believe me, then!" exclaimed the princess, astonished and angry, as she well might be.

"Did you expect me to believe you, princess?" asked the nurse coldly. "I know princesses are in the habit of telling make-believes, but you are the first I ever heard of who expected to have them believed," she added, seeing that the child was strangely in earnest.

The princess burst into tears.

"Well, I must say," remarked the nurse, now thoroughly

vexed with her for crying, "it is not at all becoming in a princess to tell stories *and* expect to be believed just because she is a princess."

"But it's quite true, I tell you."

"You've dreamed it, then, child."

"No, I didn't dream it. I went upstairs, and I lost myself, and if I hadn't found the beautiful lady, I should never have found myself."

"Oh, I daresay!"

"Well, you just come up with me and see if I'm not telling the truth."

"Indeed I have other work to do. It's your dinnertime, and I won't have any more such nonsense."

The princess wiped her eyes, and her face grew so hot that they were soon quite dry. She sat down to her dinner, but ate next to nothing. Not to be believed does not at all agree with princesses: for a real princess cannot tell a lie. So all the afternoon she did not speak a word. Only when the nurse spoke to her, she answered her, for a real princess is never rude—even when she does well to be offended.

Of course, the nurse was not comfortable in her mind—not that she suspected the least truth in Irene's story, but that she loved her dearly and was vexed with herself for having been cross to her. She thought her crossness was the cause of the princess's unhappiness, and had no idea that she was really and deeply hurt at not being believed. But, as it became more and more plain during the evening in her every motion and look that, although she tried to amuse herself with her toys, her heart was too vexed and troubled to enjoy them, her nurse's discomfort grew and grew. When bedtime came, she undressed and laid her down, but the child, instead of holding up her little mouth to be kissed, turned away from her and lay still. Then nursie's heart gave way altogether, and she began to cry. At the sound of her first sob the princess turned again, and held her face to kiss her as usual. But the nurse had her handkerchief to her eyes, and did not see the movement.

"Nursie," said the princess, "why won't you believe me?"

"Because I can't believe you," said the nurse, getting angry again.

"Ah, then, you can't help it!" said Irene. "And I will not be vexed with you anymore. I will give you a kiss and go to sleep."

"You little angel!" cried the nurse, and caught her out of bed, and walked about the room with her in her arms, kissing and hugging her.

"You *will* let me take you to see my dear old great big grandmother, won't you?" said the princess as she laid her down again.

"And *you* won't say I'm ugly anymore—will you, princess?"

"Nursie, I never said you were ugly. What can you mean?"

"Well, if you didn't say it, you meant it."

"Indeed, I never did."

"You said I wasn't so pretty as that—"

"As my beautiful grandmother—yes, I did say that; and I say it again, for it's quite true."

"Then I *do* think you *are* unkind!" said the nurse, and put her handkerchief to her eyes again.

"Nursie, dear, everybody can't be as beautiful as every other body, you know. You are *very* nice-looking, but if you had been as beautiful as my grandmother—"

"Bother your grandmother!" said the nurse.

"Nurse, that's very rude. You are not fit to be spoken to—till you can behave better."

The princess turned away once more, and again the nurse was ashamed of herself.

"I'm sure I beg your pardon, princess," she said, though still in an offended tone. But the princess let the tone pass, and heeded only the words.

"You won't say it again, I am sure," she answered, once more turning toward her nurse. "I was only going to say that if you had been twice as nice-looking as you are, some king or other would have married you, and then what would have become of me?"

"You are an angel!" repeated the nurse, again embracing her.

"Now," insisted Irene, "you *will* come and see my grand-mother—won't you?"

"I will go with you anywhere you like, my cherub," she answered, and in two minutes the weary little princess was fast asleep.

Chapter 5

The Princess Lets
Well Alone

WHEN she woke the next morning, the first thing she heard was the rain still falling. Indeed, this day was so like the last that it would have been difficult to tell where was the use of it. The first thing she thought of, however, was not the rain but the lady in the tower; and the first question that occupied her thoughts was whether she should not ask the nurse to fulfill her promise this very morning, and go with her to find her grandmother as soon as she had had her breakfast. But she came to the conclusion that perhaps the lady would not be pleased if she took anyone to see her without first asking leave, especially as it was pretty evident, seeing she lived on pigeons' eggs and cooked them herself, that she did not want the household to know she was there. So the princess resolved to take the first opportunity of running up alone and asking whether she might bring her nurse. She believed the fact that she could not otherwise convince her she was telling the truth would have much weight with her grandmother.

The princess and her nurse were the best of friends all dressing time, and the princess in consequence ate an enormous little breakfast.

"I wonder, Lootie"—that was her pet name for her nurse— "what pigeons' eggs taste like," she said as she was eating her egg—not quite a common one, for they always picked out the pinky ones for her.

"We'll get you a pigeon's egg, and you shall judge for yourself," said the nurse.

"Oh, no, no!" returned Irene, suddenly reflecting they might disturb the old lady in getting it, and that even if they did not, she would have one less in consequence.

"What a strange creature you are," said the nurse—"first to want a thing and then to refuse it!"

But she did not say it crossly, and the princess never minded any remarks that were not unfriendly.

"Well, you see, Lootie, there are reasons," she returned, and said no more, for she did not want to bring up the subject of their former strife, lest her nurse should offer to go before she had had her grandmother's permission to bring her. Of course, she could refuse to take her, but then she would believe her less than ever.

Now the nurse, as she said herself afterward, could not be every moment in the room, and as never before yesterday had the princess given her the smallest reason for anxiety, it had not yet come into her head to watch her more closely. So she soon gave her a chance, and, the very first that offered, Irene was off and up the stairs again.

This day's adventure, however, did not turn out like yesterday's, although it began like it; and indeed today is very seldom like yesterday, if people would note the differences—even when it rains. The princess ran through passage after passage, and could not find the stair of the tower. My own suspicion is that she had not gone up high enough and was searching on the second instead of the third floor. When she turned to go back, she failed equally in her search after the stair. She was lost once more.

Something made it even worse to bear this time, and it was no wonder that she cried again. Suddenly it occurred to her that it was after having cried before that she had found her grandmother's stair. She got up at once, wiped her eyes, and started upon a fresh quest. This time, although she did not find what she hoped, she found what was next best: She did not come on a stair that went up, but she came on one that went down. It was evidently not the stair she had come up, yet it was a good deal better than none, so down she went, and was singing merrily before she reached the bottom. There, to her surprise, she found herself in the kitchen. Although she was not allowed to go there alone, her nurse had often taken her, and she was a great favorite with the servants. So there was a general rush at her the moment she appeared, for everyone wanted to have her, and the report of where she was soon reached the nurse's ears. She came at once to fetch her; but she never suspected how she had got there, and the princess kept her own counsel.

Her failure to find the old lady not only disappointed her but made her very thoughtful. Sometimes she came almost to the nurse's opinion that she had dreamed all about her, but that fancy never lasted very long. She wondered much whether she should ever see her again, and thought it very sad not to have been able to find her when she particularly wanted her. She resolved to say nothing more to her nurse on the subject, seeing it was so little in her power to prove her words.

Chapter 6

The Little Miner

*T*HE next day the great cloud still hung over the mountain, and the rain poured like water from a full sponge. The princess was very fond of being out-of-doors, and she nearly cried when she saw that the weather was no better. But the mist was not of such a dark dingy gray. There was light in it, and as the hours went on it grew brighter and brighter, until it was almost too brilliant to look at.

And late in the afternoon the sun broke out so gloriously that Irene clapped her hands, crying, "See, see, Lootie! The sun has had his face washed. Look how bright he is! Do get my hat, and let us go out for a walk. Oh, dear! Oh, dear! How happy I am!"

Lootie was very glad to please the princess. She got her hat and cloak, and they set out together for a walk up the mountain, for the road was so hard and steep that the water could not rest upon it, and it was always dry enough for walking a few minutes after the rain ceased. The clouds were rolling away in broken pieces, like great, overwoolly sheep whose wool the sun had bleached till it was almost too white for the eyes to bear. Between them the sky shone with a deeper and purer blue because of the rain. The trees on the roadside were hung all over with drops, which sparkled in the sun like jewels. The only things that were no brighter for the rain were the brooks that ran down the mountain; they had changed from the clearness of crystal to a muddy brown, but what they lost in color they gained in sound—or at least in noise, for a brook when it is swollen is not so musical as before. But Irene was in raptures with the great brown streams tumbling down everywhere, and Lootie shared in her delight, for she too had been confined to the house for three days.

At length she observed that the sun was getting low, and said it was time to be going back. She made the remark again and again, but, every time, the princess begged her to go on just a little farther and a little farther, reminding her that it was much easier to go downhill, and saying that when they did turn they would be at home in a moment. So on and on they did go, now to look at a group of ferns over whose tops a stream was pouring in a watery arch, now to pick a shining stone from a rock by the wayside, now to watch the flight of some bird. Suddenly the shadow of a great mountain peak came up from behind, and shot in front of them. When the nurse saw it, she started and shook and, catching hold of the princess's hand, turned and began to run down the hill.

"What's all the haste, nursie?" asked Irene, running alongside of her.

"We must not be out a moment longer."

"But we can't help being out a good many moments longer."

It was too true. The nurse almost cried. They were much too far from home. It was against express orders to be out with the princess one moment after the sun was down, and they were nearly a mile up the mountain! If His Majesty, Irene's papa, were to hear of it, Lootie would certainly be dismissed, and to leave the princess would break her heart. It was no wonder she ran. But Irene was not in the least frightened, not knowing anything to be frightened at. She kept on chattering as well as she could, but it was not easy.

"Lootie! Lootie! Why do you run so fast? It shakes my teeth when I talk."

"Then don't talk," said Lootie.

But the princess went on talking. She was always saying: "Look, look, Lootie!" but Lootie paid no more heed to anything she said, only ran on.

"Look, look, Lootie! Don't you see that funny man peeping over the rock?"

Lootie only ran the faster. They had to pass the rock, and when they came nearer, the princess saw it was only a lump of the rock itself that she had taken for a man.

"Look, look, Lootie! There's *such* a curious creature at the foot of that old tree. Look at it, Lootie! It's making faces at us, I do think."

Lootie gave a stifled cry, and ran faster still—so fast that Irene's little legs could not keep up with her, and she fell with a crash. It was a hard downhill road, and she had been running very fast—so it was no wonder she began to cry. This put the nurse nearly beside herself, but all she could do was to run on, the moment she got the princess on her feet again.

"Who's that laughing at me?" said the princess, trying to keep in her sobs, and running too fast for her grazed knees.

"Nobody, child," said the nurse, almost angrily.

But that instant there came a burst of coarse tittering from somewhere near, and a hoarse indistinct voice that seemed to say: "Lies! Lies! Lies!"

"Oh!" cried the nurse with a sigh that was almost a scream, and ran on faster than ever.

"Nursie! Lootie! I can't run any more. Do let us walk a bit."

"What *am* I to do?" said the nurse. "Here, I will carry you."

She caught her up but found her much too heavy to run with, and had to set her down again. Then she looked wildly about her, gave a great cry, and said, "We've taken the wrong turning somewhere, and I don't know where we are. We are lost, lost!"

The terror she was in had quite bewildered her. It was true enough they had lost the way. They had been running down into a little valley in which there was no house to be seen.

Now Irene did not know what good reason there was for her nurse's terror, for the servants had all strict orders never to mention the goblins to her, but it was very discomposing to see her nurse in such a fright. Before, however, she had time to grow thoroughly alarmed like her, she heard the sound of whistling, and that revived her. Presently she saw a boy coming up the road from the valley to meet them. He was the whistler, but before they met his whistling changed to singing. And this is something like what he sang:

> *Ring! dod! bang!*
> *Go the hammers' clang!*
> *Hit and turn and bore!*
> *Whizz and puff and roar!*
> *Thus we rive the rocks,*
> *Force the goblin locks—*
> *See the shining ore!*
> *One, two, three—*
> *Bright as gold can be!*

> *Four, five, six—*
> *Shovels, mattocks, picks!*
> *Seven, eight, nine—*
> *Light your lamp at mine.*
> *Ten, eleven, twelve—*
> *Loosely hold the helve.*
> *We're the merry miner-boys,*
> *Make the goblins hold their noise.*

"I wish you would hold *your* noise," said the nurse rudely, for the very word *goblin* at such a time and in such a place made her tremble. It would bring the goblins upon them to a certainty, she thought, to defy them in that way. But whether the boy heard her or not, he did not stop his singing.

> *Thirteen, fourteen, fifteen—*
> *This is worth the siftin';*
> *Sixteen, seventeen, eighteen—*
> *There's the match, and lay't in.*
> *Nineteen, twenty—*
> *Goblins in a plenty.*

"Do be quiet," cried the nurse, in a whispered shriek. But the boy, who was now close at hand, still went on.

> *Hush! scush! scurry!*
> *There you go in a hurry!*
> *Gobble! gobble! goblin!*
> *There you go a wobblin';*
> *Hobble, hobble, hobblin'!*
> *Cobble! cobble! cobblin'!*
> *Hob-bob-goblin!—Huuuuuh!*

"There!" said the boy as he stood still opposite them. "There! That'll do for them. They can't bear singing, and they can't stand that song. They can't sing themselves, for they have no more voice than a crow, and they don't like other people to sing."

The boy was dressed in a miner's dress, with a curious cap on his head. He was a very nice-looking boy, with eyes as dark as the mines in which he worked and as sparkling as the crystals in their rocks. He was about twelve years old. His face was almost too pale for beauty, which came of his being so little in the open air and the sunlight—for even vegetables grown in the dark are white. But he looked happy, merry indeed—perhaps at the thought of having routed the goblins—and his bearing as he stood before them had nothing clownish or rude about it.

"I saw them," he went on, "as I came up, and I'm very glad I did. I knew they were after somebody, but I couldn't see who it was. They won't touch you so long as I'm with you."

"Why, who are you?" asked the nurse, offended at the freedom with which he spoke to them.

"I'm Peter's son."

"Who's Peter?"

"Peter the miner."

"I don't know him."

"I'm his son, though."

"And why should the goblins mind *you*, pray?"

"Because I don't mind them. I'm used to them."

"What difference does that make?"

"If you're not afraid of them, they're afraid of you. I'm not afraid of them. That's all. But it's all that's wanted—up here, that is. It's a different thing down there. They won't always mind that song even, down there. And if anyone sings it, they stand grinning at him awfully; and if he gets frightened, and misses a word, or says a wrong one, they—oh, don't they give it him!"

"What do they do to him?" asked Irene, with a trembling voice.

"Don't go frightening the princess," said the nurse.

"The princess!" repeated the little miner, taking off his curious cap. "I beg your pardon. But you oughtn't to be out so late. Everybody knows that's against the law."

"Yes, indeed it is!" said the nurse, beginning to cry again. "And I shall have to suffer for it."

"What does that matter?" said the boy. "It must be your fault. It is the princess who will suffer for it. I hope they didn't hear you call her the princess. If they did, they're sure to know her again: they're awfully sharp."

"Lootie! Lootie!" cried the princess. "Take me home."

"Don't go on like that," said the nurse to the boy, almost fiercely. "How could I help it? I lost my way."

"You shouldn't have been out so late. You wouldn't have lost your way if you hadn't been frightened," said the boy. "Come along. I'll soon set you right again. Shall I carry your little Highness?"

"Impertinence!" murmured the nurse, but she did not say it aloud, for she thought if she made him angry he might take his revenge by telling someone belonging to the house, and then it would be sure to come to the king's ears.

"No, thank you," said Irene. "I can walk very well, though I can't run so fast as nursie. If you will give me one hand, Lootie will give me another, and then I shall get on famously."

They soon had her between them, holding a hand each.

"Now let's run," said the nurse.

"No, no," said the little miner. "That's the worst thing you can do. If you hadn't run before, you would not have lost your way. And if you run now, they will be after you in a moment."

"I don't want to run," said Irene.

"You don't think of *me*," said the nurse.

"Yes, I do, Lootie. The boy says they won't touch us if we don't run."

"Yes, but if they know at the house that I've kept you out so late I shall be turned away, and that would break my heart."

"Turned away, Lootie! Who would turn you away?"

"Your papa, child."

"But I'll tell him it was all my fault. And you know it was, Lootie."

"He won't mind that. I'm sure he won't."

"Then I'll cry, and go down on my knees to him, and beg him not to take away my own dear Lootie."

The nurse was comforted at hearing this, and said no more. They went on, walking pretty fast, but taking care not to run a step.

"I want to talk to you," said Irene to the little miner, "but it's so awkward! I don't know your name."

"My name's Curdie, little princess."

"What a funny name! Curdie! What more?"

"Curdie Peterson. What's your name, please?"

"Irene."

"What more?"

"I don't know what more. What more is my name, Lootie?"

"Princesses haven't got more than one name. They don't want it."

"Oh, then, Curdie, you must call me just Irene and no more."

"No, indeed," said the nurse indignantly. "He shall do no such thing."

"What shall he call me, then, Lootie?"

"Your Royal Highness."

"My Royal Highness! What's that? No, no, Lootie. I won't be called names. I don't like them. You told me once yourself it's only rude children that call names, and I'm sure Curdie wouldn't be rude. Curdie, my name's Irene."

"Well, Irene," said Curdie, with a glance at the nurse which showed he enjoyed teasing her, "it is very kind of you to let me call you anything. I like your name very much."

He expected the nurse to interfere again, but he soon saw that she was too frightened to speak. She was staring at something a few yards before them in the middle of the path, where it narrowed between rocks so that only one could pass at a time.

"It is very much kinder of you to go out of your way to take us home," said Irene.

"I'm not going out of my way yet," said Curdie. "It's on the other side of those rocks the path turns off to my father's."

"You wouldn't think of leaving us till we're safe home, I'm sure," gasped the nurse.

"Of course not," said Curdie.

"You dear, good, kind Curdie! I'll give you a kiss when we get home," said the princess.

The nurse gave her a great pull by the hand she held. But at that instant the something in the middle of the way, which had looked like a great lump of earth brought down by the rain, began to move. One after another it shot out four long things, like two arms and two legs, but it was now too dark to tell what they were. The nurse began to tremble from head to foot. Irene clasped Curdie's hand yet faster, and Curdie began to sing again:

> *One, two—*
> *Hit and hew!*
> *Three, four—*
> *Blast and bore!*

> *Five, six—*
> *There's a fix!*
> *Seven, eight—*
> *Hold it straight!*
> *Nine, ten—*
> *Hit again!*
> *Hurry! scurry!*
> *Bother! smother!*
> *There's a toad*
> *In the road!*
> *Smash it!*
> *Squash it!*
> *Fry it!*
> *Dry it!*
> *You're another!*
> *Up and off!*
> *There's enough!—Huuuuuh!"*

As he uttered the last words, Curdie let go his hold of his companion, and rushed at the thing in the road as if he would trample it under his feet. It gave a great spring, and ran straight up one of the rocks like a huge spider. Curdie turned back laughing, and took Irene's hand again. She grasped his very tight, but said nothing till they had passed the rocks. A few yards more and she found herself on a part of the road she knew, and was able to speak again.

"Do you know, Curdie, I don't quite like your song. It sounds to me rather rude," she said.

"Well, perhaps it is," answered Curdie. "I never thought of that; it's a way we have. We do it because they don't like it."

"Who don't like it?"

"The cobs, as we call them."

"Don't!" said the nurse.

"Why not?" said Curdie.

"I beg you won't. Please don't."

"Oh! If you ask me that way, of course I won't, though I don't a bit know why. Look! There are the lights of your great house down below. You'll be at home in five minutes now."

Nothing more happened. They reached home in safety. Nobody had missed them, or even known they had gone out, and they arrived at the door belonging to their part of the house without anyone seeing them. The nurse was rushing in with a hurried and not overgracious good-night to Curdie, but the princess pulled her hand from hers, and was just throwing her arms round Curdie's neck, when she caught her again and dragged her away.

"Lootie! Lootie! I promised a kiss," said Irene.

"A princess mustn't give kisses. It's not at all proper," said Lootie.

"But I promised," said the princess.

"There's no occasion; he's only a miner-boy."

"He's a good boy, and a brave boy, and he has been very kind to us. Lootie! Lootie! I *promised.*"

"Then you shouldn't have promised."

"Lootie, I promised him a kiss."

"Your Royal Highness," said Lootie, suddenly grown very respectful, "must come in directly."

"Nurse, a princess must *not* break her word," said Irene, drawing herself up and standing stock-still.

Lootie did not know which the king might count the worse—to let the princess be out after sunset, or to let her kiss a miner-boy. She did not know that, being a gentleman, as many kings have been, he would have counted neither of them the worse. However much he might have disliked his daughter to kiss the miner-boy, he would not have had her break her word for all the goblins in creation. But, as I say, the nurse was not lady enough to understand this, and so she was in a great difficulty, for, if she insisted, someone might hear the princess cry and run to see, and then all would come out. But here Curdie came again to the rescue.

"Never mind, Princess Irene," he said. "You mustn't kiss me tonight. But you shan't break your word. I will come another time. You may be sure I will."

"Oh, thank you, Curdie!" said the princess, and stopped crying.

"Good night, Irene; good night, Lootie," said Curdie, and turned and was out of sight in a moment.

"I should like to see him!" muttered the nurse as she carried the princess to the nursery.

"You *will* see him," said Irene. "You may be sure Curdie will keep his word. He's *sure* to come again."

"I should like to see him!" repeated the nurse, and said no more. She did not want to open a new cause of strife with the princess by saying more plainly what she meant. Glad enough that she had succeeded both in getting home unseen and in keeping the princess from kissing the miner-boy, she resolved to watch her far better in future. Her carelessness had already doubled the danger she was in. Formerly the goblins were her only fear; now she had to protect her charge from Curdie as well.

Chapter 7

The Mines

CURDIE went home whistling. He resolved to say nothing about the princess for fear of getting the nurse into trouble, for while he enjoyed teasing her because of her absurdity, he was careful not to do her any harm. He saw no more of the goblins, and was soon fast asleep in his bed.

He woke in the middle of the night, and thought he heard curious noises outside. He sat up and listened, then got up and, opening the door very quietly, went out. When he peeped round the corner, he saw, under his own window, a group of stumpy creatures, whom he at once recognized by their shape. Hardly, however, had he begun his "One, two, three!" when they broke asunder, scurried away, and were out of sight. He returned laughing, got into bed again, and was fast asleep in a moment.

Reflecting a little over the matter in the morning, he came to the conclusion that, as nothing of the kind had ever happened before, they must be annoyed with him for interfering to protect the princess. By the time he was dressed, however, he

was thinking of something quite different, for he did not value
the enmity of the goblins in the least.

As soon as they had breakfast, he set off with his father for
the mine.

They entered the hill by a natural opening under a huge
rock, where a little stream rushed out. They followed its course
for a few yards, when the passage took a turn, and sloped
steeply into the heart of the hill. With many angles and wind-
ings and branchings-off, and sometimes with steps where it
came upon a natural gulf, it led them deep into the hill before
they arrived at the place where they were at present digging out
the precious ore. This was of various kinds, for the mountain
was very rich in the better sorts of metals. With flint and steel,
and tinderbox, they lighted their lamps, then fixed them on
their heads, and were soon hard at work with their pickaxes
and shovels and hammers. Father and son were at work near
each other, but not in the same gang—the passages out of
which the ore was dug, they called gangs—for when the lode,
or vein of ore, was small, one miner would have to dig away
alone in a passage no bigger than gave him just room to
work—sometimes in uncomfortable cramped positions. If they
stopped for a moment they could hear everywhere around them,
some nearer, some farther off, the sounds of their companions
burrowing away in all directions in the inside of the great
mountain—some boring holes in the rock in order to blow it up
with gunpowder, others shoveling the broken ore into baskets
to be carried to the mouth of the mine, others hitting away
with their pickaxes. Sometimes, if the miner was in a very
lonely part, he would hear only a tap-tapping, no louder than
that of a woodpecker, for the sound would come from a great
distance off through the solid mountain rock.

The work was hard at best, for it is very warm underground, but it was not particularly unpleasant, and some of the miners, when they wanted to earn a little more money for a particular purpose, would stop behind the rest and work all night. But you could not tell night from day down there, except from feeling tired and sleepy, for no light of the sun ever came into those gloomy regions. Some who had thus remained behind during the night, although certain there were none of their companions at work, would declare the next morning that they heard, every time they halted for a moment to take breath, a tap-tapping all about them, as if the mountain were then more full of miners than ever it was during the day; and some in consequence would never stay overnight, for all knew those were the sounds of the goblins. They worked only at night, for the miners' night was the goblins' day. Indeed, the greater number of the miners were afraid of the goblins, for there were strange stories well known amongst them of the treatment some had received whom the goblins had surprised at their work during the night. The more courageous of them, however, amongst them Peter Peterson and Curdie, who in this took after his father, had stayed in the mine all night again and again, and although they had several times encountered a few stray goblins, had never yet failed in driving them away. As I have indicated already, the chief defense against them was verse, for they hated verse of every kind, and some kinds they could not endure at all. I suspect they could not make any themselves, and that was why they disliked it so much. At all events, those who were most afraid of them were those who could neither make verses themselves nor remember the verses that other people made for them; while those who were never afraid were those who could make verses for themselves, for although there

were certain old rhymes which were very effectual, yet it was
well known that a new rhyme, if of the right sort, was even
more distasteful to them, and therefore more effectual in putting them to flight.

Perhaps my readers may be wondering what the goblins could
be about, working all night long, seeing they never carried up
the ore and sold it, but when I have informed them concerning
what Curdie learned the very next night, they will be able to
understand.

For Curdie had determined, if his father would permit him,
to remain there alone this night—and that for two reasons:
First, he wanted to get extra wages that he might buy a very
warm red petticoat for his mother, who had begun to complain
of the cold of the mountain air sooner than usual this autumn;
and second, he had just a faint hope of finding out what the
goblins were about under his window the night before.

When he told his father, he made no objection, for he had
great confidence in his boy's courage and resources.

"I'm sorry I can't stay with you," said Peter, "but I want to go
and pay the parson a visit this evening, and besides I've had a
bit of a headache all day."

"I'm sorry for that, Father," said Curdie.

"Oh, it's not much! You'll be sure to take care of yourself,
won't you?"

"Yes, Father, I will. I'll keep a sharp lookout, I promise you."

Curdie was the only one who remained in the mine. About
six o'clock the rest went away, everyone bidding him good
night, and telling him to take care of himself, for he was a great
favorite with them all.

"Don't forget your rhymes," said one.

"No, no," answered Curdie.

"It's no matter if he does," said another, "for he'll only have to make a new one."

"Yes, but he mightn't be able to make it fast enough," said another, "and while it was cooking in his head, they might take a mean advantage and set upon him."

"I'll do my best," said Curdie. "I'm not afraid."

"We all know that," they returned, and left him.

Chapter 8

The Goblins

*F*OR some time Curdie worked away briskly, throwing all the ore he had disengaged on one side behind him, to be ready for carrying out in the morning. He heard a good deal of goblin-tapping, but it all sounded far away in the hill, and he paid it little heed. Toward midnight he began to feel rather hungry; so he dropped his pickax, got out a lump of bread which in the morning he had laid in a damp hole in the rock, sat down on a heap of ore, and ate his supper. Then he leaned back for five minutes' rest before beginning his work again, and laid his head against the rock. He had not kept the position for one minute before he heard something which made him sharpen his ears. It sounded like a voice inside the rock. After a while he heard it again. It was a goblin voice—there could be no doubt about that—and this time he could make out the words.

"Hadn't we better be moving?" it said.

A rougher and deeper voice replied, "There's no hurry. That wretched little mole won't be through tonight, if he work ever so hard. He's not by any means at the thinnest place."

"But you still think the lode does come through into our house?" said the first voice.

"Yes, but a good bit farther on than he has got to yet. If he had struck a stroke more to the side just here," said the goblin, tapping the very stone, as it seemed to Curdie, against which his head lay, "he would have been through, but he's a couple of yards past it now, and if he follow the lode it will be a week before it leads him in. You see it back there—a long way. Still, perhaps, in case of accident it would be as well to be getting out of this. Helfer, you'll take the great chest. That's your business, you know."

"Yes, Dad," said a third voice. "But you must help me to get it on my back. It's awfully heavy, you know."

"Well, it isn't just a bag of smoke, I admit. But you're as strong as a mountain, Helfer."

"You say so, Dad. I think myself I'm all right. But I could carry ten times as much if it wasn't for my feet."

"That *is* your weak point, I confess, my boy."

"Ain't it yours too, Father?"

"Well, to be honest, it is a goblin weakness. Why *they* come so soft, I declare I haven't an idea."

"Specially when your head's so hard, you know, Father."

"Yes, my boy. The goblin's glory is his head. To think how the fellows up above there have to put on helmets and things when they go fighting! Ha! Ha!"

"But why don't we wear shoes like them, Father? I should like it—especially when I've got a chest like that on my head."

"Well, you see, it's not the fashion. The king never wears shoes."

"The queen does."

"Yes, but that's for distinction. The first queen, you see—I mean the king's first wife—wore shoes, of course, because she came from upstairs, and so, when she died, the next queen would not be inferior to her as she called it, and would wear shoes too. It was all pride. She is the hardest in forbidding them to the rest of the women."

"I'm sure I wouldn't wear them—no, not for—that I wouldn't!" said the first voice, which was evidently that of the mother of the family. "I can't think why either of them should."

"Didn't I tell you the first was from upstairs?" said the other. "That was the only silly thing I ever knew His Majesty guilty of. Why should he marry an outlandish woman like that—one of our natural enemies too?"

"I suppose he fell in love with her."

"Pooh! Pooh! He's just as happy now with one of his own people."

"Did she die *very* soon? They didn't tease her to death, did they?"

"Oh, dear, no! The king worshiped her very footmarks."

"What made her die, then? Didn't the air agree with her?"

"She died when the young prince was born."

"How silly of her! *We* never do that. It must have been because she wore shoes."

"I don't know that."

"Why do they wear shoes up there?"

"Ah, now that's a sensible question, and I will answer it. But in order to do so, I must first tell you a secret. I once saw the queen's feet."

"Without her shoes?"

"Yes—without her shoes."

"No! Did you? How was it?"

"Never you mind how it was. *She* didn't know I saw them. And what do you think! They had *toes*!"

"Toes! What's that?"

"You may well ask! I should never have known if I had not seen the queen's feet. Just imagine! The ends of her feet were split up into five or six thin pieces!"

"Oh, horrid! How *could* the king have fallen in love with her?"

"You forget that she wore shoes. That is just why she wore them. That is why all the men, and women too, upstairs wear shoes. They can't bear the sight of their own feet without them."

"Ah, now I understand! If ever you wish for shoes again, Helfer, I'll hit your feet—I will."

"No, no, Mother, pray don't."

"Then don't you."

"But with such a big box on my head—"

A horrid scream followed, which Curdie interpreted as in reply to a blow from his mother upon the feet of her eldest goblin.

"Well, I never knew so much before!" remarked a fourth voice.

"Your knowledge is not universal quite yet," said the father. "You were only fifty last month. Mind you see to the bed and bedding. As soon as we've finished our supper, we'll be up and going. Ha! Ha! Ha!"

"What are you laughing at, husband?"

"I'm laughing to think what a mess the miners will find themselves in—somewhere before this day ten years."

"Why, what do you mean?"

"Oh, nothing."

"Oh, yes, you do mean something. You always do mean something."

"It's more than you do, then, wife."

"That may be, but it's not more than I find out, you know."

"Ha! Ha! You're a sharp one. What a mother you've got, Helfer!"

"Yes, Father."

"Well, I suppose I must tell you. They're all at the palace consulting about it tonight, and as soon as we've got away from this thin place I'm going there to hear what night they fix upon. I should like to see that young ruffian there on the other side, struggling in the agonies of—"

He dropped his voice so low that Curdie could hear only a growl. The growl went on in the low bass for a good while, as inarticulate as if the goblin's tongue had been a sausage, and it was not until his wife spoke again that it rose to its former pitch.

"But what shall we do when you are at the palace?" she asked.

"I will see you safe in the new house I've been digging for you for the last two months. Podge, you mind the table and chairs. I commit them to your care. The table has seven legs—each chair three. I shall require them all at your hands."

After this arose a confused conversation about the various household goods and their transport, and Curdie heard nothing more that was of any importance.

He now knew at least one of the reasons for the constant sound of the goblin hammers and pickaxes at night. They were making new houses for themselves, to which they might retreat when the miners should threaten to break into their dwellings. But he had learned two things of far greater importance. The first was, that some grievous calamity was preparing, and almost ready to fall upon the heads of the miners; the second was—the one weak point of a goblin's body. He had not known that their feet were so tender as he had now reason to suspect. He had heard it said that they had no toes: he had never had opportunity of inspecting them closely enough, in the dusk in which they always appeared, to satisfy himself whether it was a correct report. Indeed, he had not been able even to satisfy himself as to whether they had no fingers, although that also was commonly said to be the fact. One of the miners, indeed, who had had more schooling than the rest, was wont to argue that such must have been the primordial condition of humanity, and that education and handicraft had developed both toes and fingers—with which proposition Curdie had once heard his father sarcastically agree, alleging in support of it the probability that babies' gloves were a traditional remnant of the old state of things, while the stockings of all ages, no regard being paid in them to the toes, pointed in the same direction. But what was of importance was the fact concerning the softness of the goblin feet, which he foresaw might be useful to all miners. What he had to do in the meantime, however, was to discover, if possible, the special evil design the goblins had now in their heads.

Although he knew all the gangs and all the natural galleries with which they communicated in the mined part of the mountain, he had not the least idea where the palace of the king of the gnomes was, otherwise he would have set out at once on the enterprise of discovering what the said design was. He judged, and rightly, that it must lie in a farther part of the mountain, between which and the mine there was as yet no communication. There must be one nearly completed, however, for it could be but a thin partition which now separated them. If only he could get through in time to follow the goblins as they retreated! A few blows would doubtless be sufficient—just where his ear now lay; but if he attempted to strike there with his pickax, he would only hasten the departure of the family, put them on their guard, and perhaps lose their involuntary guidance. He therefore began to feel the wall with his hands, and soon found that some of the stones were loose enough to be drawn out with little noise.

Laying hold of a large one with both his hands, he drew it gently out, and let it down softly.

"What was that noise?" said the goblin father.

Curdie blew out his light, lest it should shine through.

"It must be that one miner that stayed behind the rest," said the mother.

"No, he's been gone a good while. I haven't heard a blow for an hour. Besides, it wasn't like that."

"Then I suppose it must have been a stone carried down the brook inside."

"Perhaps. It will have more room by and by."

Curdie kept quite still. After a little while, hearing nothing but the sounds of their preparations for departure, mingled with an occasional word of direction, and anxious to know whether the removal of the stone had made an opening into the goblins' house, he put in his hand to feel. It went in a good way, and then came in contact with something soft. He had but a moment to feel it over, it was so quickly withdrawn: it was one of the toeless goblin feet. The owner of it gave a cry of fright.

"What's the matter, Helfer?" asked his mother.

"A beast came out of the wall and licked my foot."

"Nonsense! There are no wild beasts in our country," said his father.

"But it was, Father. I felt it."

"Nonsense, I say. Will you malign your native realms and reduce them to a level with the country upstairs? That is swarming with wild beasts of every description."

"But I did feel it, Father."

"I tell you to hold your tongue. You are no patriot."

Curdie suppressed his laughter, and lay still as a mouse—but no stiller, for every moment he kept nibbling away with his fingers at the edge of the hole. He was slowly making it bigger, for here the rock had been very much shattered with the blasting.

There seemed to be a good many in the family, to judge from the mass of confused talk which now and then came through the hole; but when all were speaking together, and just as if they had bottle brushes—each at least one—in their throats, it was not easy to make out much that was said. At length he heard once more what the father goblin was saying.

"Now, then," he said, "get your bundles on your backs. Here, Helfer, I'll help you up with your chest."

"I wish it *was* my chest, Father."

"Your turn will come in good time enough! Make haste. I *must* go to the meeting at the palace tonight. When that's over, we can come back and clear out the last of the things before our enemies return in the morning. Now light your torches, and come along. What a distinction it is to provide our own light, instead of being dependent on a thing hung up in the air—a most disagreeable contrivance—intended no doubt to blind us when we venture out under its baleful influence! Quite glaring and vulgar, I call it, though no doubt useful to poor creatures who haven't the wit to make light for themselves!"

Curdie could hardly keep himself from calling through to know whether they made the fire to light their torches by. But a moment's reflection showed him that they would have said they did, inasmuch as they struck two stones together, and the fire came.

Chapter 9

The Hall of the Goblin Palace

A SOUND of many soft feet followed, but soon ceased. Then Curdie flew at the hole like a tiger, and tore and pulled. The sides gave way, and it was soon large enough for him to crawl through. He would not betray himself by rekindling his lamp, but the torches of the retreating company, which he found departing in a straight line up a long avenue from the door of their cave, threw back light enough to afford him a glance round the deserted home of the goblins. To his surprise, he could discover nothing to distinguish it from an ordinary natural cave in the rock, upon many of which he had come with the rest of the miners in the progress of their excavations.

The goblins had talked of coming back for the rest of their household gear: he saw nothing that would have made him suspect a family had taken shelter there for a single night. The floor was rough and stony; the walls full of projecting corners;

the roof in one place twenty feet high, in another endangering his forehead; while on one side a stream, no thicker than a needle, it is true, but still sufficient to spread a wide dampness over the wall, flowed down the face of the rock. But the troop in front of him was toiling under heavy burdens. He could distinguish Helfer now and then, in the flickering light and shade, with his heavy chest on his bending shoulders, while the second brother was almost buried in what looked like a great feather bed. "Where do they get the feathers?" thought Curdie. But in a moment the troop disappeared at a turn of the way, and it was now both safe and necessary for Crudie to follow them, lest they should be round the next turning before he saw them again, for so he might lose them altogether. He darted after them like a greyhound. When he reached the corner and looked cautiously round, he saw them again at some distance down another long passage. None of the galleries he saw that night bore signs of the work of man—or of goblin either. Stalactites, far older than the mines, hung from their roofs, and their floors were rough with boulders and large round stones, showing that there water must have once run. He waited again at this corner till they had disappeared round the next, and so followed them a long way through one passage after another. The passages grew more and more lofty, and were more and more covered in the roof with shining stalactites.

It was a strange enough procession which he followed. But the strangest part of it was the household animals which crowded amongst the feet of the goblins. It was true they had no wild animals down there—at least they did not know of any, but they had a wonderful number of tame ones. I must, however, reserve any contributions toward the natural history of these for a later position in my story.

At length, turning a corner too abruptly, he had almost rushed into the middle of the goblin family; for there they had already set down all their burdens on the floor of a cave considerably larger than that which they had left. They were as yet too breathless to speak, else he would have had warning of their arrest. He started back, however, before anyone saw him, and retreating a good way, stood watching till the father should come out to go to the palace. Before very long, both he and his son Helfer appeared and kept on in the same direction as before, while Curdie followed them again with renewed precaution. For a long time he heard no sound except something like the rush of a river inside the rock, but at length what seemed the far-off noise of a great shouting reached his ears, which, however, presently ceased. After advancing a good way farther, he thought he heard a single voice. It sounded clearer and clearer as he went on, until at last he could almost distinguish the words. In a moment or two, keeping after the goblins round another corner, he once more started back—this time in amazement.

He was at the entrance of a magnificent cavern, of an oval shape, once probably a huge natural reservoir of water, now the great palace hall of the goblins. It rose to a tremendous height, but the roof was composed of such shining materials, and the multitude of torches carried by the goblins who crowded the floor lighted up the place so brilliantly, that Curdie could see to the top quite well. But he had no idea how immense the place was until his eyes had got accustomed to it, which was not for a good many minutes. The rough projections on the walls, and the shadows thrown upward from them by the torches, made the sides of the chamber look as if they were crowded with statues upon brackets and pedestals, reaching in irregular tiers from floor to roof. The walls themselves were, in many parts, of gloriously shining substances, some of them gorgeously colored besides, which powerfully contrasted with the shadows. Curdie could not help wondering whether his rhymes would be of any use against such a multitude of goblins as filled the floor of the hall, and indeed felt considerably tempted to begin his shout of "One, two, three!" But as there was no reason for routing them, and much for endeavoring to discover their designs, he kept himself perfectly quiet, and peeping round the edge of the doorway, listened with both his sharp ears.

At the other end of the hall, high above the heads of the multitude, was a terrace-like ledge of considerable height, caused by the receding of the upper part of the cavern wall. Upon this sat the king and his court, the king on a throne hollowed out of a huge block of green copper ore, and his court upon lower seats around it. The king had been making them a speech, and the applause which followed it was what Curdie had heard. One of the court was now addressing the multitude. What he heard him say was to the following effect:

"Hence it appears that two plans have been for some time together working in the strong head of His Majesty for the deliverance of his people. Regardless of the fact that we were the first possessors of the regions they now inhabit, regardless equally of the fact that we abandoned that region from the loftiest motives; regardless also of the self-evident fact that we excel them so far in mental ability as they excel us in stature, they look upon us as a degraded race, and make a mockery of all our finer feelings. But the time has almost arrived when— thanks to His Majesty's inventive genius—it will be in our power to take a thorough revenge upon them once for all, in respect of their unfriendly behavior."

"May it please Your Majesty—" cried a voice close by the door, which Curdie recognized as that of the goblin he had followed.

"Who is he that interrupts the Chancellor?" cried another from near the throne.

"Glump," answered several voices.

"He is our trusty subject," said the king himself, in a slow and stately voice. "Let him come forward and speak."

A lane was parted through the crowd, and Glump, having ascended the platform and bowed to the king, spoke as follows:

"Sire, I would have held my peace, had I not known that I only knew how near was the moment to which the Chancellor had just referred. In all probability, before another day is past, the enemy will have broken through into my house—the partition between being even now not more than a foot in thickness."

"Not quite so much," thought Curdie to himself.

"This very evening I have had to remove my household effects, therefore the sooner we are ready to carry out the plan, for the execution of which His Majesty has been making such magnificent preparations, the better. I may just add, that within the last few days I have perceived a small outbreak in my dining room, which, combined with observations upon the course of the river escaping where the evil men enter, has convinced me that close to the spot must lie a deep gulf in its channel. This discovery will, I trust, add considerably to the otherwise immense forces at His Majesty's disposal."

He ceased, and the king graciously acknowledged his speech with a bend of his head, whereupon Glump, after a bow to His Majesty, slid down amongst the rest of the undistinguished multitude. Then the Chancellor rose and resumed.

"The information which the worthy Glump has given us," he

said, "might have been of considerable import at the present
moment, but for that other design already referred to, which
naturally takes precedence. His Majesty, unwilling to proceed
to extremities, and well aware that such measures sooner or
later result in violent reactions, has excogitated a more funda-
mental and comprehensive measure, of which I need say no
more. Should His Majesty be successful—as who dares to doubt?
—then a peace, all to the advantage of the goblin kingdom,
will be established for a generation at least, rendered absolutely
secure by the pledge which His Royal Highness the prince will
have and hold for the good behavior of her relatives. Should
His Majesty fail—which who shall dare even to imagine in his
most secret thoughts?—then will be the time for carrying out
with rigor the design to which Glump referred, and for which
our preparations are even now all but completed. The failure of
the former will render the latter imperative."

Curdie, perceiving that the assembly was drawing to a close
and that there was little chance of either plan being more fully
discovered, now thought it prudent to make his escape before
the goblins began to disperse, and slipped quietly away.

There was not much danger of meeting any goblins, for all
the men at least were left behind him in the the palace, but
there was considerable danger of his taking a wrong turning, for
he had now no light and had therefore to depend upon his
memory and his hands. After he had left behind him the glow
that issued from the door of Glump's new abode, he was utterly
without guide, so far as his eyes were concerned.

He was most anxious to get back through the hole before the
goblins should return to fetch the remains of their furniture. It
was not that he was in the least afraid of them, but, as it was of
the utmost importance that he should thoroughly discover what

the plans they were cherishing were, he must not occasion the slightest suspicion that they were watched by a miner.

He hurried on, feeling his way along the walls of rock. Had he not been very courageous, he must have been very anxious, for he could not but know that if he lost his way it would be the most difficult thing in the world to find it again. Morning would bring no light into these regions; and toward him least of all, who was known as a special rhymester and persecutor, could goblins be expected to exercise courtesy. Well might he wish that he had brought his lamp and tinderbox with him, of which he had not thought when he crept so eagerly after the goblins! He wished it all the more when, after a while, he found his way blocked up, and could get no farther. It was of no use to turn back, for he had not the least idea where he had begun to go wrong. Mechanically, however, he kept feeling about the walls that hemmed him in. His hand came upon a place where a tiny stream of water was running down the face of the rock. "What a stupid I am!" he said to himself. "I am actually at the end of my journey! And there are the goblins coming back to fetch their things!" he added as the red glimmer of their torches appeared at the end of the long avenue that led up to the cave. In a moment he had thrown himself on the floor, and wriggled backward through the hole. The floor on the other side was several feet lower, which made it easier to get back. It was all he could do to lift the largest stone he had taken out of the hole, but he did manage to shove it in again. He sat down on the ore heap and thought.

He was pretty sure that the latter plan of the goblins was to inundate the mine by breaking outlets for the water accumulated in the natural reservoirs of the mountains, as well as running through portions of it. While the part hollowed by the miners remained shut off from that inhabited by the goblins, they had had no opportunity of injuring them thus; but now that a passage was broken through, and the goblins' part proved the higher in the mountain, it was clear to Curdie that the mine could be destroyed in an hour. Water was always the chief danger to which the miners were exposed. They met with a little chokedamp sometimes, but never with the explosive fire-damp so common in coal mines. Hence they were careful as soon as they saw any appearance of water.

As the result of his reflections while the goblins were busy in their old home, it seemed to Curdie that it would be best to build up the whole of this gang, filling it with stone, and clay or lime, so that there should be no smallest channel for the water to get into. There was not, however, any immediate danger, for the execution of the goblins' plan was contingent upon the failure of that unknown design which was to take precedence of it. And he was most anxious to keep the door of communication open, that he might if possible discover what the former plan was. At the same time, they could not resume their intermitted labors for the inundation without his finding it out, when by putting all hands to the work, the one existing outlet might in a single night be rendered impenetrable to any weight of water, for by filling the gang entirely up, their embankment would be buttressed by the sides of the mountain itself.

As soon as he found that the goblins had again retired, he lighted his lamp, and proceeded to fill the hole he had made with such stones as he could withdraw when he pleased. He then thought it better, as he might have occasion to be up a good many nights after this, to go home and have some sleep.

How pleasant the night air felt upon the outside of the

mountain after what he had gone through in the inside of it! He hurried up the hill without meeting a single goblin on the way, and called and tapped at the window until he woke his father, who soon rose and let him in. He told him the whole story, and, just as he had expected, his father thought it best to work that lode no farther, but at the same time to pretend occasionally to be at work there still in order that the goblins might have no suspicions. Both father and son then went to bed and slept soundly until the morning.

Chapter 10

The Princess's King-papa

*T*HE weather continued fine for weeks, and the little princess went out every day. So long a period of fine weather had indeed never been known upon that mountain. The only uncomfortable thing was that her nurse was so nervous and particular about being in before the sun was down that often she would take to her heels when nothing worse than a fleecy cloud crossing the sun threw a shadow on the hillside; and many an evening they were home a full hour before the sunlight had left the weathercock on the stables. If it had not been for such odd behavior Irene would by this time have almost forgotten the goblins. She never forgot Curdie, but him she remembered for his own sake, and indeed would have remembered him if only because a princess never forgets her debts until they are paid.

One splendid sunshiny day, about an hour after noon, Irene, who was playing on a lawn in the garden, heard the distant blast of a bugle. She jumped up with a cry of joy, for she knew by that particular blast that her father was on his way to see her. This part of the garden lay on the slope of the hill and allowed a full view of the country below. So she shaded her eyes with her hand and looked far away to catch the first glimpse of shining armor. In a few moments a little troop came glittering round the shoulder of a hill. Spears and helmets were sparkling and gleaming, banners were flying, horses prancing, and again came the bugle blast which was to her like the voice of her father calling across the distance: "Irene, I'm coming." On and on they came until she could clearly distinguish the king. He rode a white horse and was taller than any of the men with him. He wore a narrow circle of gold set with jewels around his helmet, and as he came still nearer Irene could discern the flashing of the stones in the sun. It was a long time since he had been to see her, and her little heart beat faster and faster as the shining troop approached, for she loved her king-papa very dearly and was nowhere so happy as in his arms. When they reached a certain point, after which she could see them no more from the garden, she ran to the gate, and there stood till up they came clanging and stamping with one more bright bugle blast which said: "Irene, I am come."

By this time the people of the house were all gathered at the gate, but Irene stood alone in front of them. When the horsemen pulled up she ran to the side of the white horse and held up her arms. The king stooped and took her hands. In an instant she was on the saddle and clasped in his great strong arms. I wish I could describe the king so that you could see him in your mind. He had gentle blue eyes, but a nose that made him look like an eagle. A long dark beard, streaked with silvery lines, flowed from his mouth almost to his waist, and as Irene sat on the saddle and hid her glad face upon his bosom it mingled with the golden hair which her mother had given her, and the two together were like a cloud with streaks of the sun woven through it. After he had held her to his heart for a minute he spoke to his white horse, and the beautiful creature, which had been prancing so proudly a little while before, walked as gently as a lady—for he knew he had a little lady on his back— through the gate and up to the door of the house. Then the king set her on the ground and, dismounting, took her hand and walked with her into the great hall, which was hardly ever entered except when he came to see his little princess. There he sat down, with two of his councillors who had accompanied him, to have some refreshment, and Irene sat on his right hand and drank her milk out of a wooden bowl curiously carved.

After the king had eaten and drunk he turned to the princess and said, stroking her hair, "Now, my child, what shall we do next?"

This was the question he almost always put to her first after their meal together, and Irene had been waiting for it with some impatience, for now, she thought, she should be able to settle a question which constantly perplexed her.

"I should like you to take me to see my great old grandmother."

The king looked grave and said, "What does my little daughter mean?"

"I mean the Queen Irene that lives up in the tower—the very old lady, you know, with the long hair of silver."

The king only gazed at his little princess with a look which she could not understand.

"She's got her crown in her bedroom," she went on, "but I've not been in there yet. You know she's there, don't you?"

"No," said the king, very quietly.

"Then it must all be a dream," said Irene. "I half thought it was, but I couldn't be sure. Now I *am* sure of it. Besides, I couldn't find her the next time I went up."

At that moment a snow-white pigeon flew in at an open window and settled upon Irene's head. She broke into a merry laugh, cowered a little, and put up her hands to her head, saying, "Dear dovey, don't peck me. You'll pull out my hair with your long claws if you don't mind."

The king stretched out his hand to take the pigeon, but it spread it wings and flew again through the open window, when its whiteness made one flash in the sun and vanished. The king laid his hand on his princess's head, held it back a little, gazed in her face, smiled half a smile, and sighed half a sigh.

"Come, my child. We'll have a walk in the garden together," he said.

"You won't come up and see my huge, great beautiful grandmother, then, King-papa?" said the princess.

"Not this time," said the king very gently. "She has not invited me, you know, and great old ladies like her do not choose to be visited without leave asked and given."

The garden was a very lovely place. Being upon a mountainside there were parts in it where the rocks came through in great masses, and all immediately about them remained quite wild. Tufts of heather grew upon them, and other hardy mountain plants and flowers, while near them would be lovely roses and lilies and all pleasant garden flowers. This mingling of the wild mountain with the civilized garden was very quaint, and it was impossible for any number of gardeners to make such a garden look formal and stiff.

Against one of these rocks was a garden seat, shadowed from the afternoon sun by the overhanging of the rock itself. There was a little winding path up to the top of the rock, and on top another seat; but they sat on the seat at its foot because the sun was hot, and there they talked together of many things.

At length the king said, "You were out late one evening, Irene."

"Yes, Papa. It was my fault; and Lootie was very sorry."

"I must talk to Lootie about it," said the king.

"Don't speak loud to her, please, Papa," said Irene. "She's been so afraid of being late ever since! Indeed she has not been naughty. It was only a mistake for once."

"Once might be too often," murmured the king to himself as he stroked his child's head.

I can't tell you how he had come to know. I am sure Curdie had not told him. Someone about the palace must have seen them, after all. He sat for a good while thinking. There was no sound to be heard except that of a little stream which ran merrily out of an opening in the rock by where they sat, and sped away down the hill through the garden. Then he rose and, leaving Irene where she was, went into the house and sent for Lootie, with whom he had a talk that made her cry.

When in the evening he rode away upon his great white horse, he left six of his attendants behind him, with orders that three of them should watch outside the house every night, walking round and round it from sunset to sunrise. It was clear he was not quite comfortable about the princess.

Chapter 11

The Old Lady's Bedroom

NOTHING more happened worth telling for some time. The autumn came and went by. There were no more flowers in the garden. The wind blew strong, and howled among the rocks. The rain fell, and drenched the few yellow and red leaves that could not get off the bare branches. Again and again there would be a glorious morning followed by a pouring afternoon, and sometimes, for a week together, there would be rain, nothing but rain, all day, and then the most lovely cloudless night, with the sky all out in full-blown stars—not one missing. But the princess could not see much of them, for she went to bed early. The winter drew on, and she found things growing dreary. When it was too stormy to go out, and she had got tired of her toys, Lootie would take her about the house, sometimes to the housekeeper's room, where the housekeeper, who was a good, kind old woman, made much of her—sometimes to the servants' hall or the kitchen, where she was not princess merely, but absolute queen, and ran a great risk of being spoiled. Sometimes she would run off herself to the

room where the men-at-arms whom the king had left sat, and
they showed her their arms and accoutrements, and did what
they could to amuse her. Still at times she found it very dreary,
and often and often wished that her huge great grandmother had
not been a dream.

One morning the nurse left her with the housekeeper for a
while. To amuse her, she turned out the contents of an old
cabinet upon the table. The little princess found her treasures,
queer ancient ornaments, and many things the use of which she
could not imagine, far more interesting than her own toys, and
sat playing with them for two hours or more. But, at length, in
handling a curious old-fashioned brooch, she ran the pin of it
into her thumb, and gave a little scream with the sharpness of
the pain, but would have thought little more of it had not the
pain increased and her thumb begun to swell. This alarmed the
housekeeper greatly. The nurse was fetched, the doctor was
sent for, her hand was poulticed, and long before her usual
time she was put to bed. The pain still continued, and although
she fell asleep and dreamed a good many dreams, there was the
pain always in every dream. At last it woke her up.

The moon was shining brightly into the room. The poultice
had fallen off her hand and it was burning hot. She fancied if
she could hold it into the moonlight, that would cool it. So she
got out of bed, without waking the nurse, who lay at the other
end of the room, and went to the window. When she looked
out she saw one of the men-at-arms walking in the garden with
the moonlight glancing on his armor. She was just going to tap
on the window and call him, for she wanted to tell him all
about it, when she bethought herself that that might wake
Lootie, and she would put her into her bed again. So she
resolved to go to the window of another room, and call him from

there. It was so much nicer to have somebody to talk to than to lie awake in bed with the burning pain in her hand. She opened the door very gently and went through the nursery, which did not look into the garden, to go to the other window. But when she came to the foot of the old staircase there was the moon shining down from some window high up, and making the worm-eaten oak look very strange and delicate and lovely. In a moment she was putting her little feet one after the other in the silvery path up the stair, looking behind as she went, to see the shadow they made in the middle of the silver. Some little girls would have been afraid to find themselves thus along in the middle of the night, but Irene was a princess.

As she went slowly up the stair, not quite sure that she was not dreaming, suddenly a great longing woke up in her heart to try once more whether she could not find the old lady with the silvery hair.

"If she is a dream," she said to herself, "then I am the likelier to find her, if I am dreaming."

So up and up she went, stair after stair, until she came to the many rooms—all just as she had seen them before. Through passage after passage she softly sped, comforting herself that if she should lose her way it would not matter much, because when she woke she would find herself in her own bed with Lootie not far off. But, as if she had known every step of the way, she walked straight to the door at the foot of the narrow stair that led to the tower.

"What if I should realliality-really find my beautiful old grandmother up there!" she said to herself as she crept up the steep steps.

When she reached the top she stood a moment listening in the dark, for there was no moon there. Yes, it was! It was the hum of the spinning wheel! What a diligent grandmother to work both day and night!

She tapped gently at the door.

"Come in, Irene," said the sweet voice.

The princess opened the door and entered. There was the moonlight streaming in at the window, and in the middle of the moonlight sat the old lady in her black dress with the white lace, and her silvery hair mingling with the moonlight, so that you could not have told which was which.

"Come in, Irene," she said again. "Can you tell me what I am spinning?"

"She speaks," thought Irene, "just as if she had seen me five minutes ago, or yesterday at the farthest." "No," she answered, "I don't know what you are spinning. Please, I thought you were a dream. Why couldn't I find you before, Great-great-grandmother?"

"That you are hardly old enough to understand. But you would have found me sooner if you hadn't come to think I was a dream. I will give you one reason, though, why you couldn't find me. I didn't want you to find me."

"Why, please?"

"Because I did not want Lootie to know I was here."

"But you told me to tell Lootie."

"Yes. But I knew Lootie would not believe you. If she were to see me sitting spinning here, she wouldn't believe me either."

"Why?"

"Because she couldn't. She would rub her eyes, and go away and say she felt queer, and forget half of it and more, and then say it had been all a dream."

"Just like me," said Irene, feeling very much ashamed of herself.

"Yes, a good deal like you, but not just like you, for you've come again; and Lootie wouldn't have come again. She would have said, No, no—she had had enough of such nonsense."

"Is it naughty of Lootie, then?"

"It would be naughty of you. I've never done anything for Lootie."

"And you did wash my face and hands for me," said Irene, beginning to cry.

The old lady smiled a sweet smile and said, "I'm not vexed with you, my child—nor with Lootie either. But I don't want you to say anything more to Lootie about me. If she should ask you, you must just be silent. But I do not think she will ask you."

All the time they talked the old lady kept on spinning.

"You haven't told me yet what I am spinning," she said.

"Because I don't know. It's very pretty stuff."

It was indeed very pretty stuff. There was a good bunch of it on the distaff attached to the spinning wheel, and in the moonlight it shone like—what shall I say it was like? It was not white enough for silver—yes, it was like silver, but shone gray rather than white, and glittered only a little. And the thread the old lady drew out from it was so fine that Irene could hardly see it.

"I am spinning this for you, my child."

"For me! What am I to do with it, please?"

"I will tell you by and by. But first I will tell you what it is. It is spiderwebs—of a particular kind. My pigeons bring it me from over the great sea. There is only one forest where the spiders live who make this particular kind—the finest and strongest of any. I have nearly finished my present job. What is on the rock now will be enough. I have a week's work there yet, though," she added, looking at the bunch.

"Do you work all day and all night, too, Great-great-great-great-grandmother?" said the princess, thinking to be very polite with so many *greats*.

"I am not quite so great as all that," she answered, smiling almost merrily. "If you call me grandmother, that will do. No, I don't work every night—only moonlit nights, and then no longer than the moon shines upon my wheel. I shan't work much longer tonight."

"And what will you do next, Grandmother?"

"Go to bed. Would you like to see my bedroom?"

"Yes, that I should."

"Then I think I won't work any longer tonight. I shall be in good time."

The old lady rose, and left her wheel standing just as it was. You see, there was no good in putting it away, for where there was not any furniture there was no danger of being untidy.

Then she took Irene by the hand, but it was her bad hand and Irene gave a little cry of pain.

"My child!" said her grandmother. "What is the matter?"

Irene held her hand into the moonlight, that the old lady might see it, and told her all about it, at which she looked grave. But she only said, "Give me your other hand," and, having led her out upon the little dark landing, opened the door on the opposite side of it. What was Irene's surprise to see the loveliest room she had ever seen in her life! It was large and lofty, and dome-shaped. From the center hung a lamp as round as a ball, shining as if with the brightest moonlight, which made everything visible in the room, though not so clearly that the princess could tell what many of the things were. A large oval bed stood in the middle, with a coverlid of rose color, and velvet curtains all round it of a lovely pale blue. The walls were also blue—spangled all over with what looked like stars of silver.

The old lady left her and, going to a strange-looking cabinet, opened it and took out a curious silver casket. Then she sat down on a low chair and, calling Irene, made her kneel before her while she looked at her hand. Having examined it, she opened the casket, and took from it a little ointment. The sweetest odor filled the room—like that of roses and lilies—as she rubbed the ointment gently all over the hot swollen hand. Her touch was so pleasant and cool that it seemed to drive away the pain and heat wherever it came.

"Oh, Grandmother! It is *so* nice!" said Irene. "Thank you, thank you."

Then the old lady went to a chest of drawers, and took out a large handkerchief of gossamer-like cambric, which she tied round her hand.

"I don't think I can let you go away tonight," she said. "Would you like to sleep with me?"

"Oh, yes, yes, dear Grandmother!" said Irene, and would have clapped her hands, forgetting that she could not.

"You won't be afraid, then, to go to bed with such an old woman?"

"No. You are so beautiful, Grandmother."

"But I am *very* old."

"And I suppose I am very young. You won't mind sleeping with such a *very* young woman, Grandmother?"

"You sweet little pertness!" said the old lady, and drew her toward her, and kissed her on the forehead and the cheek and the mouth.

Then she got a large silver basin, and having poured some water into it made Irene sit on the chair, and washed her feet.

This done, she was ready for bed. And oh, what a delicious bed it was into which her grandmother laid her! She hardly could have told she was lying upon anything: she felt nothing but the softness. The old lady, having undressed herself, lay down beside her.

"Why don't you put out your moon?" asked the princess.

"That never goes out, night or day," she answered. "In the darkest night, if any of my pigeons are out on a message, they always see my moon and know where to fly to."

"But if somebody besides the pigeons were to see it—somebody about the house, I mean—they would come to look what it was and find you."

"The better for them, then," said the old lady. "But it does not happen above five times in a hundred years that anyone does see it. The greater part of those who do take it for a meteor, wink their eyes, and forget it again. Besides, nobody could find the room except I pleased. Besides, again—I will tell you a secret—if that light were to go out you would fancy yourself lying in a bare garret, on a heap of old straw, and would not see one of the pleasant things round about you all the time."

"I hope it will never go out," said the princess.

"I hope not. But it is time we both went to sleep. Shall I take you in my arms?"

The little princess nestled close up to the old lady, who took her in both her arms and held her close to her bosom.

"Oh, dear! This is so nice!" said the princess. "I didn't know anything in the world could be so comfortable. I should like to lie here forever."

"You may if you will," said the old lady. "But I must put you to one trial—not a *very* hard one, I hope. This night week you must come back to me. If you don't, I do not know when you may find me again, and you will soon want me very much."

"Oh, please, don't let me forget!"

"You shall not forget. The only question is whether you will believe I am anywhere—whether you will believe I am anything but a dream. You may be sure I will do all I can to help you to come. But it will rest with yourself, after all. On the night of next Friday, you must come to me. Mind, now."

"I *will* try," said the princess.

"Then good night," said the old lady, and kissed the forehead which lay in her bosom.

In a moment more the little princess was dreaming in the midst of the loveliest dreams—of summer seas and moonlight and mossy springs and great murmuring trees, and beds of wild flowers with such odors as she had never smelled before. But, after all, no dream could be more lovely than what she had left behind when she fell asleep.

In the morning she found herself in her own bed. There was no handkerchief or anything else on her hand, only a sweet odor lingered about it. The swelling had all gone down, the prick of the brooch had vanished—in fact, her hand was perfectly well.

Chapter 12

A Short Chapter About Curdie

CURDIE spent many nights in the mine. His father and he had taken Mrs. Peterson into the secret, for they knew Mother could hold her tongue, which was more than could be said of all the miners' wives. But Curdie did not tell her that every night he spent in the mine, part of it went in earning a new red petticoat for her.

Mrs. Peterson was such a nice good mother! All mothers are nice and good more or less, but Mrs. Peterson was nice and good all *more* and no *less*. She made and kept a little heaven in that poor cottage on the high hillside—for her husband and son to go home to out of the low and rather dreary earth in which they worked. I doubt if the princess was very much happier even in the arms of her huge great-grandmother than Peter and Curdie were in the arms of Mrs. Peterson. True, her hands were hard and chapped and large, but it was with work for them; and therefore, in the sight of the angels, her hands were so much the more beautiful. And if Curdie worked hard to get her a petticoat, she worked hard every day to get him comforts which he would have missed much more than she would a new petticoat even in winter. Not that she and Curdie ever thought of how much they worked for each other: that would have spoiled everything.

When left alone in the mine Curdie always worked on for an hour or two at first, following the lode which, according to Glump, would lead at last into the deserted habitation. After that, he would set out on a reconnoitering expedition. In order to manage this, or rather the return from it, better than the first time, he had bought a huge ball of fine string, having learned the trick from Hop-o'-my-Thumb, whose history his mother had often told him. Not that Hop-o'-my-Thumb had ever used a ball of string—I should be sorry to be supposed so far out in my classics—but the principle was the same as that of the pebbles. The end of this string he fastened to his pickax, which figured no bad anchor, and then, with the ball in his hand, unrolling it as he went, set out in the dark through the natural gangs of the goblins' territory. The first night or two he came upon nothing worth remembering; saw only a little of the home life of the cobs in the various caves they called houses; failed in coming upon anything to cast light upon the foregoing design which kept the inundation for the present in the background. But at length, I think on the third or fourth night, he found, partly guided by the noise of their implements, a company of evidently the best sappers and miners amongst them, hard at work. What were they about? It could not well be the inundation, seeing that had in the meantime been postponed to something else. Then what was it? He lurked and watched, every now and then in the greatest risk of being detected, but without success. He had again and again to retreat in haste, a proceeding rendered the more difficult that he had to gather up his string as he returned upon its course. It was not that he was afraid of the goblins, but that he was afraid of their finding out that they were watched, which might have prevented the discovery at which he aimed. Sometimes his haste had to be such that, when he reached home toward morning, his string, for lack of time to wind it up as he "dodged the cobs," would be in what seemed most hopeless entanglement; but after a good sleep, though a short one, he always found his mother had got it right again. There it was, wound in a most respectable ball, ready for use the moment he should want it!

"I can't think how you do it, Mother," he would say.

"I follow the thread," she would answer, "just as you do in the mine."

She never had more to say about it, but the less clever she was with her words, the more clever she was with her hands; and the less his mother said, the more Curdie believed she had to say.

But still he had made no discovery as to what the goblin miners were about.

Chapter 13

The Cobs' Creatures

ABOUT this time the gentlemen whom the king had left behind him to watch over the princess had each occasion to doubt the testimony of his own eyes, for more than strange were the objects to which they would bear witness. They were of one sort—creatures—but so grotesque and mis-shapen as to be more like a child's drawings upon his slate than anything natural. They saw them only at night, while on guard about the house. The testimony of the man who first reported having seen one of them was that, as he was walking slowly round the house, while yet in the shadow, he caught sight of a creature standing on its hind legs in the moonlight, with its forefeet upon a window ledge, staring in at the window. Its body might have been that of a dog or wolf, he thought, but he declared on his honor that its head was twice the size it ought to have been for the size of its body, and as round as a ball, while the face, which it turned upon him as it fled, was more like one carved by a boy upon the turnip inside which he is going to put a candle than anything else he could think of. It rushed into the garden. He sent an arrow after it, and thought he must have struck it, for it gave an unearthly howl, and he could not find his arrow any more than the beast, although he searched all about the place where it vanished.

They laughed at him until he was driven to hold his tongue, and said he must have taken too long a pull at the ale jug. But before two nights were over he had one to side with him, for he, too, had seen something strange, only quite different from that reported by the other. The description the second man gave of the creature he had seen was yet more grotesque and unlikely. They were both laughed at by the rest; but night after night another came over to their side, until at last there was only one left to laugh at all his companions. Two nights more passed, and he saw nothing; but on the third he came rushing from the garden to the other two before the house, in such an agitation that they declared—for it was their turn now—that the band of his helmet was cracking under his chin with the rising of his hair inside it.

Running with him into that part of the garden which I have already described, they saw a score of creatures, to not one of which they could give a name, and not one of which was like another, hideous and ludicrous at once, gamboling on the lawn in the moonlight. The supernatural or rather subnatural ugliness of their faces, the length of legs and necks in some, the apparent absence of both or either in others, made the spectators, although in one consent as to what they saw, yet doubtful, as I have said, of the evidence of their own eyes—and ears as well; for the noises they made, although not loud, were as uncouth and varied as their forms, and could be described neither as grunts nor squeaks nor roars nor howls nor barks nor yells nor screams nor croaks nor hisses nor mews nor shrieks, but only as something like all of them mingled in one horrible dissonance. Keeping in the shade, the watchers had a few moments to recover themselves before the hideous assembly suspected their presence; but all at once, as if by common consent, they scampered off in the direction of a great rock, and vanished before the men had come to themselves sufficiently to think of following them.

My readers will suspect what these were, but I will now give them full information concerning them. They were, of course, household animals belonging to the goblins, whose ancestors had taken their ancestors many centuries before from the upper regions of light into the lower regions of darkness. The original stocks of these horrible creatures were very much the same as the animals now seen about farms and homes in the country, with the exception of a few of them, which had been wild creatures, such as foxes, and indeed wolves and small bears, which the goblins, from their proclivity toward the animal creation, had caught when cubs and tamed. But in the course of time all had undergone even greater changes than had passed upon their owners. They had altered—that is, their descendants had altered—into such creatures as I have not attempted to describe except in the vaguest manner, the various parts of their bodies assuming, in an apparently arbitrary and self-willed manner, the most abnormal developments. Indeed, so little did any distinct type predominate in some of the bewildering results, that you could only have guessed at any known animal as the original, and even then, what likeness remained would be more one of general expression than of definable conformation.

But what increased the gruesomeness tenfold was that, from constant domestic, or indeed rather family association with the goblins, their countenances had grown in grotesque resem-

blance to the human. No one understands animals who does
not see that every one of them, even amongst the fishes, it may
be with a dimness and vagueness infinitely remote, yet shadows
the human: in the case of these the human resemblance had
greatly increased: while their owners had sunk toward them,
they had risen toward their owners. But the conditions of
subterranean life being equally unnatural for both, while the
goblins were worse, the creatures had not improved by the
approximation, and its result would have appeared far more
ludicrous than consoling to the warmest lover of animal nature.
I shall now explain how it was that just then these animals
began to show themselves about the king's country house.

The goblins, as Curdie had discovered, were mining on—at
work both day and night, in divisions, urging the scheme after
which he lay in wait. In the course of their tunneling they had
broken into the channel of a small stream, but the break being
in the top of it, no water had escaped to interfere with their
work. Some of the creatures, hovering as they often did about
their masters, had found the hole, and had, with the curiosity
which had grown to a passion from the restraints of their
unnatural circumstances, proceeded to explore the channel.
The stream was the same which ran out by the seat on which
Irene and her king-papa had sat as I have told, and the goblin
creatures found it jolly fun to get out for a romp on a smooth
lawn such as they had never seen in all their poor miserable
lives. But although they had partaken enough of the nature of
their owners to delight in annoying and alarming any of the
people whom they met on the mountain, they were, of course,
incapable of designs of their own, or of intentionally furthering
those of their masters.

For several nights after the men-at-arms were at length of

one mind as to the fact of the visits of some horrible creatures, whether bodily or spectral they could not yet say, they watched with special attention that part of the garden where they had last seen them. Perhaps indeed they gave in consequence too little attention to the house. But the creatures were too cunning to be easily caught, nor were the watchers quick-eyed enough to descry the head, or the keen eyes in it, which, from the opening whence the stream issued, would watch them in turn, ready, the moment they should leave the lawn, to report the place clear.

Chapter 14

That Night Week

*D*URING the whole of the week Irene had been thinking every other moment of her promise to the old lady, although even now she could not feel quite sure that she had not been dreaming. Could it really be that an old lady lived up in the top of the house, with pigeons and a spinning wheel, and a lamp that never went out? She was, however, none the less determined, on the coming Friday, to ascend the three stairs, walk through the passages with the many doors, and try to find the tower in which she had either seen or dreamed her grandmother.

Her nurse could not help wondering what had come to the child—she would sit so thoughtfully silent, and even in the midst of a game with her would so suddenly fall into a dreamy mood. But Irene took care to betray nothing, whatever efforts Lootie might make to get at her thoughts. And Lootie had to say to herself, "What an odd child she is!" and give it up.

At length the longed-for Friday arrived, and lest Lootie should be moved to watch her, Irene endeavored to keep herself as quiet as possible. In the afternoon she asked for her dollhouse, and went on arranging and rearranging the various rooms and their inhabitants for a whole hour. Then she gave a sigh and threw herself back in her chair. One of the dolls would not sit, and another would not stand, and they were all very tiresome. Indeed, there was one would not even lie down, which was too bad. But it was now getting dark, and the darker it got the more excited Irene became, and the more she felt it necessary to be composed.

"I see you want your tea, princess," said the nurse. "I will go and get it. The room feels close: I will open the window a little. The evening is mild. It won't hurt you."

"There's no fear of that, Lootie," said Irene, wishing she had put off going for the tea till it was darker, when she might have made her attempt with every advantage.

I fancy Lootie was longer in returning than she had intended, for when Irene, who had been lost in thought, looked up, she saw it was nearly dark, and at the same moment caught sight of a pair of eyes, bright with a green light, glowering at her through the open window. The next instant something leaped into the room. It was like a cat, with legs as long as a horse's, Irene said, but its body no bigger and its legs no thicker than those of a cat. She was too frightened to cry out, but not too frightened to jump from her chair and run from the room.

It is plain enough to every one of my readers what she ought to have done—and indeed Irene thought of it herself. But when she came to the foot of the old stair, just outside the nursery door, she imagined the creature running up those long ascents after her, and pursuing her through the dark passages—*which, after all, might lead to no tower*! That thought was too much. Her heart failed her, and turning from the stair, she rushed along to the hall, whence, finding the front door open, she darted into the court pursued—at least she thought so—by the creature. No one happening to see her, on she ran, unable to think for fear, and ready to run anywhere to elude the awful creature with the stilt legs. Not daring to look behind her, she rushed straight out of the gate and up the mountain. It was foolish indeed—thus to run farther and farther from all who could help her, as if she had been seeking a fit spot for the goblin creature to eat her in at his leisure, but that is the way fear serves us: It always sides with the thing we are afraid of.

The princess was soon out of breath with running uphill, but she ran on, for she fancied the horrible creature just behind her, forgetting that, had it been after her, such long legs as those must have overtaken her long ago. At last she could run no longer, and fell, unable even to scream, by the roadside, where she lay for some time half dead with terror. But finding nothing lay hold of her, and her breath beginning to come back, she ventured at length to get half up and peer anxiously about her. It was now so dark she could see nothing. Not a single star was out. She could not even tell in what direction the house lay, and between her and home she fancied the dreadful creature lying ready to pounce upon her. She saw now that she ought to have run up the stairs at once. It was well she did not scream, for although very few of the goblins had come out for weeks, a stray idler or two might have heard her. She sat down upon a stone, and nobody but one who had done something wrong could have been more miserable. She had quite forgotten her promise to visit her grandmother. A raindrop fell on her face. She looked up, and for a moment her terror was lost in astonishment. At first she thought the rising moon had left her place and drawn nigh to see what could be the matter with the little girl, sitting alone, without hat or cloak, on the dark bare mountain; but she soon saw she was mistaken, for there was no light on the ground at her feet, and no shadow anywhere. But a great silvery globe was hanging in the air, and as she gazed at the lovely thing, her courage revived. If she were but indoors again, she would fear nothing, not even the terrible creature with the long legs! But how was she to find her way back? What could that light be? Could it be—? No, it couldn't. But what if it should be—yes—it must be—her great-great-grandmother's lamp, which guided her pigeons home through the darkest night! She jumped up: she had but to keep that light in view and she must find the house.

Her heart grew strong. Speedily, yet softly, she walked down the hill, hoping to pass the watching creature unseen. Dark as it was, there was little danger now of choosing the wrong road. And—which was most strange—the light that filled her eyes from the lamp, instead of blinding them for a moment to the object upon which they next fell, enabled her for a moment to see it, despite the darkness. By looking at the lamp and then dropping her eyes, she could see the road for a yard or two in front of her, and this saved her from several falls, for the road was very rough. But all at once, to her dismay, it vanished, and the terror of the beast, which had left her the moment she began to return, again laid hold of her heart. The same instant, however, she caught the light of the windows, and knew exactly where she was. It was too dark to run, but she made what haste she could, and reached the gate in safety. She found the house door still open, ran through the hall, and, without even looking into the nursery, bounded straight up the stair, and the next, and the next, then turning to the right, ran through the

long avenue of silent rooms, and found her way at once to the
door at the foot of the tower stair.

When first the nurse missed her, she fancied she was playing
her a trick, and for some time took no trouble about her, but at
last, getting frightened, she had begun to search; and when the
princess entered, the whole household was hither and thither
over the house, hunting for her. A few seconds after she
reached the stair of the tower they had even begun to search
the neglected rooms, in which they would never have thought
of looking had they not already searched every other place they
could think of in vain. But by this time she was knocking at the
old lady's door.

Chapter 15

Woven and Then Spun

"COME in, Irene," said the silvery voice of her grandmother.

The princess opened the door and peeped in. But the room was quite dark and there was no sound of the spinning wheel. She grew frightened once more, thinking that, although the room was there, the old lady might be a dream after all. Every little girl knows how dreadful it is to find a room empty where she thought somebody was; but Irene had to fancy for a moment that the person she came to find was nowhere at all. She remembered, however, that at night she spun only in the moonlight, and concluded that must be why there was no sweet, beelike humming: the old lady might be somewhere in the darkness.

Before she had time to think another thought, she heard her voice again, saying as before, "Come in, Irene."

From the sound, she understood at once that she was not in the room beside her. Perhaps she was in her bedroom. She turned across the passage, feeling her way to the other door.

When her hand fell on the lock, again the old lady spoke. "Shut the other door behind you, Irene. I always close the door of my workroom when I go to my chamber."

Irene wondered to hear her voice so plainly through the door: having shut the other, she opened it and went in. Oh, what a lovely haven to reach from the darkness and fear through which she had come! The soft light made her feel as if she were going into the heart of the milkiest pearl; while the blue walls and their silver stars for a moment perplexed her with the fancy that they were in reality the sky which she had left outside a minute ago covered with rainclouds.

"I've lighted a fire for you, Irene: you're cold and wet," said her grandmother.

Then Irene looked again, and saw that what she had taken for a huge bouquet of red roses on a low stand against the wall was in fact a fire which burned in the shapes of the loveliest and reddest roses, glowing gorgeously between the heads and wings of two cherubs of shining silver. And when she came nearer, she found that the smell of roses with which the room was filled came from the fire roses on the hearth. Her grandmother was dressed in the loveliest pale blue velvet, over which her hair, no longer white, but of a rich golden color, streamed like a cataract, here falling in dull gathered heaps, there rushing away in smooth shining falls. And ever as she looked, the hair seemed pouring down from her head and vanishing in a golden mist ere it reached the floor. It flowed from under the edge of a circle of shining silver, set with alternated pearls and opals. On her dress was no ornament whatever, neither was there a ring on her hand, or a necklace or carcanet about her neck. But her slippers glimmered with the light of the Milky

Way, for they were covered with seed pearls and opals in one mass. Her face was that of a woman of three and twenty.

The princess was so bewildered with astonishment and admiration that she could hardly thank her, and drew nigh with timidity, feeling dirty and uncomfortable. The lady was seated on a low chair by the side of the fire, with hands outstretched to take her, but the princess hung back with a troubled smile.

"Why, what's the matter?" asked her grandmother. "You haven't been doing anything wrong—I know that by your face, though it *is* rather miserable. What's the matter, my dear?"

And she still held out her arms.

"Dear Grandmother," said Irene, "I'm not so sure that I haven't done something wrong. I ought to have run up to you at once when the long-legged cat came in at the window, instead of running out on the mountain and making myself such a fright."

"You were taken by surprise, my child, and are not so likely to do it again. It is when people do wrong things willfully that they are the more likely to do them again. Come."

And still she held out her arms.

"But Grandmother, you're so beautiful and grand with your crown on, and I am so dirty with mud and rain! I should quite spoil your beautiful blue dress."

With a merry little laugh the lady sprang from her chair, more lightly far than Irene herself could, caught the child to her bosom, and, kissing the tearstained face over and over, sat down with her in her lap.

"Oh, Grandmother, you'll make yourself such a mess!" cried Irene, clinging to her.

"You darling! Do you think I care more for my dress than for my little girl? Besides—look here."

As she spoke she set her down, and Irene saw to her dismay that the lovely dress was covered with the mud of her fall on the mountain road. But the lady stooped to the fire, and taking from it, by the stalk in her fingers, one of the burning roses, passd it once and again and a third time over the front of her dress; and when Irene looked, not a single stain was to be discovered.

"There!" said her grandmother, "you won't mind coming to me now?"

But Irene again hung back, eying the flaming rose which the lady held in her hand.

"You're not afraid of the rose—are you?" she said, about to throw it on the hearth again.

"Oh, don't please!" cried Irene. "Won't you hold it to my frock and my hands and my face? And I'm afraid my feet and my knees want it too!"

"No," answered her grandmother, smiling a little sadly as she threw the rose from her, "it is too hot for you yet. It would set *your* frock in a flame. Besides, I don't want to make you clean tonight. I want your nurse and the rest of the people to see you as you are, for you will have to tell them how you ran away for fear of the long-legged cat. I should like to wash you, but they would not believe you then. Do you see that bath behind you?"

The princess looked, and saw a large oval tub of silver, shining brilliantly in the light of the wonderful lamp.

"Go and look into it," said the lady.

Irene went, and came back very silent with her eyes shining.

"What did you see?" asked her grandmother.

"The sky and the moon and the stars," she answered. "It looked as if there was no bottom to it."

The lady smiled a pleased satisfied smile, and was silent also for a few moments. Then she said, "Any time you want a bath, come to me. I know you have a bath every morning, but sometimes you want one at night, too."

"Thank you, Grandmother, I will—I will indeed," answered Irene, and was again silent for some moments thinking. Then she said, "How was it, Grandmother, that I saw your beautiful lamp—not the light of it only—but the great round silvery lamp itself, hanging alone in the great open air, high up? It was your lamp I saw—wasn't it?"

"Yes, my child, it was my lamp."

"Then how was it? I don't see a window all round."

"When I please I can make the lamp shine through the walls—shine so strong that it melts them away from before the sight, and shows itself as you saw it. But, as I told you, it is not everybody can see it."

"How is it that I can, then? I'm sure I don't know."

"It is a gift born with you. And one day I hope everybody will have it."

"But how do you make it shine through the walls?"

"Ah! That you would not understand if I were to try ever so much to make you—not yet—not yet. But," added the lady, rising, "you must sit in my chair while I get you the present I have been preparing for you. I told you my spinning was for you. It is finished now, and I am going to fetch it. I have been keeping it warm under one of my brooding pigeons."

Irene sat down in the low chair, and her grandmother left her, shutting the door behind her. The child sat gazing, now at the rose fire, now at the starry walls, now at the silver light, and a great quietness grew in her heart. If all the long-legged cats in the world had come rushing at her then, she would not have been afraid of them for a moment. How this was she could not tell—she only knew there was no fear in her, and every-thing was so right and safe that it could not get in.

She had been gazing at the lovely lamp for some minutes fixedly: turning her eyes, she found the wall had vanished, for she was looking out on the dark cloudy night. But though she heard the wind blowing, none of it blew upon her. In a moment more the clouds themselves parted, or rather vanished like the wall, and she looked straight into the starry herds, flashing gloriously in the dark blue. It was but for a moment. The clouds gathered again and shut out the stars, the wall gathered again and shut out the clouds, and there stood the lady beside her with the loveliest smile on her face, and a shimmering ball in her hand, about the size of a pigeon's egg.

"There, Irene, there is my work for you!" she said, holding out the ball to the princess.

She took it in her hand, and looked at it all over. It sparkled a little, and shone here and there, but not much. It was of a sort of gray-whiteness, something like spun glass.

"Is this *all* your spinning, Grandmother?" she asked.

"All since you came to the house. There is more there than you think."

"How pretty it is! What am I to do with it, please?"

"That I will now explain to you," answered the lady, turning from her and going to her cabinet.

She came back with a small ring in her hand. Then she took the ball from Irene's, and did something with the two—Irene could not tell what.

"Give me your hand," she said.

Irene held up her right hand.

"Yes, that is the hand I want," said the lady, and put the ring on the forefinger of it.

"What a beautiful ring!" said Irene. "What is the stone called?"

"It is a fire opal."

"Please, am I to keep it?"

"Always."

"Oh, thank you, Grandmother! It's prettier than anything I ever saw, except those—of all colors—in your— Please, is that your crown?"

"Yes, it is my crown. The stone in your ring is of the same sort—only not so good. It has only red, but mine have all colors, you see."

"Yes, Grandmother. I will take such care of it! But—" she added, hesitating.

"But what?" asked her grandmother.

"What am I to say when Lootie asks me where I got it?"

"*You* will ask *her* where you got it," answered the lady, smiling.

"I don't see how I can do that."

"You will, though."

"Of course I will, if you say so. But, you know, I can't pretend not to know."

"Of course not. But don't trouble yourself about it. You will see when the time comes."

So saying, the lady turned, and threw the little ball into the rose fire.

"Oh, Grandmother!" exclaimed Irene, "I thought you had spun it for me."

"So I did, my child. And you've got it."

"No, it's burnt in the fire!"

The lady put her hand in the fire, brought out the ball, glimmering as before, and held it toward her. Irene stretched out her hand to take it, but the lady turned and, going to her cabinet, opened a drawer, and laid the ball in it.

"Have I done anything to vex you, Grandmother?" said Irene pitifully.

"No, my darling. But you must understand that no one ever gives anything to another properly and really without keeping it. That ball is yours."

"Oh! I'm not to take it with me! You are going to keep it for me!"

"You are to take it with you. I've fastened the end of it to the ring on your finger."

Irene looked at the ring.

"I can't see it there, Grandmother," she said.

"Feel—a little way from the ring—toward the cabinet," said the lady.

"Oh! I do feel it!" exclaimed the princess. "But I can't see it," she added, looking close to her outstretched hand.

"No. The thread is too fine for you to see it. You can only feel it. Now you can fancy how much spinning that took, although it does seem such a little ball."

"But what use can I make of it, if it lies in your cabinet?"

"That is what I will explain to you. It would be of no use to you—it wouldn't be yours at all if it did not lie in my cabinet. Now listen. If ever you find yourself in any danger—such, for example, as you were in this same evening—you must take off your ring and put it under the pillow of your bed. Then you must lay your forefinger, the same that wore the ring, upon the thread, and follow the thread wherever it leads you."

"Oh, how delightful! It will lead me to you, Grandmother, I know!"

"Yes. But, remember, it may seem to you a very roundabout

way indeed, and you must not doubt the thread. Of one thing you may be sure, that while you hold it, I hold it too."

"It is very wonderful!" said Irene thoughtfully. Then suddenly, becoming aware, she jumped up, crying, "Oh, Grandmother! Here have I been sitting all this time in your chair, and you standing! I *beg* your pardon."

The lady laid her hand on her shoulder, and said, "Sit down again, Irene. Nothing pleases me better than to see anyone sit in my chair. I am only too glad to stand so long as anyone will sit in it."

"How kind of you!" said the princess, and sat down again.

"It makes me happy," said the lady.

"But," said Irene, still puzzled, "won't the thread get in somebody's way and be broken, if the one end is fast to my ring, and the other laid in your cabinet?"

"You will find all that arrange itself. I am afraid it is time for you to go."

"Mightn't I stay and sleep with you tonight, Grandmother?"

"No, not tonight. If I had meant you to stay tonight, I should have given you a bath; but you know everybody in the house is miserable about you, and it would be cruel to keep them so all night. You must go downstairs."

"I'm so glad, Grandmother, you didn't say, "Go home," for this is my home. Mayn't I call this my home?"

"You may, my child. And I trust you will always think it your home. Now come. I must take you back without anyone seeing you."

"Please, I want to ask you one question more," said Irene. "Is it because you have your crown on that you look so young?"

"No, child," answered her grandmother, "it is because I felt

so young this evening that I put my crown on. And I thought
you would like to see your old grandmother at her best."

"Why do you call yourself old? You're not old, Grandmother."

"I am very old indeed. It is so silly of people—I don't mean
you, for you are such a tiny, and couldn't know better—but it is
so silly of people to fancy that old age means crookedness and
witheredness and feebleness and sticks and spectacles and rheu-
matism and forgetfulness! It is so silly! Old age has nothing
whatever to do with all that. The right old age means strength
and beauty and mirth and courage and clear eyes and strong
painless limbs. I am older than you are able to think, and—"

"And look at you, Grandmother!" cried Irene, jumping up
and flinging her arms about her neck. "I won't be so silly again,
I promise you. At least—I'm rather afraid to promise—but if I
am, I promise to be sorry for it—I do. I wish I were as old as
you, Grandmother. I don't think you are ever afraid of anything."

"Not for long, at least, my child. Perhaps by the time I am
two thousand years of age, I shall, indeed, never be afraid of
anything. But I confess I have sometimes been afraid about my
children—sometimes about you, Irene."

"Oh, I'm so sorry, Grandmother! Tonight, I suppose, you
mean."

"Yes—a little tonight, but a good deal when you had all but
made up your mind that I was a dream, and no real great-great-
grandmother. You must not suppose I am blaming you for that.
I daresay you could not help it."

"I don't know, Grandmother," said the princess, beginning
to cry. "I can't always do myself as I should like. And I don't
always try. I'm very sorry anyhow."

The lady stooped, lifted her in her arms, and sat down with
her in her chair, holding her close to her bosom. In a few

minutes the princess had sobbed herself to sleep. How long she slept, I do not know. When she came to herself she was sitting in her own high chair at the nursery table, with her dollhouse before her.

Chapter 16

The Ring

*T*HE same moment her nurse came into the room, sobbing. When she saw her sitting there she started back with a loud cry of amazement and joy. Then running to her, she caught her in her arms and covered her with kisses.

"My precious darling princess! Where have you been? What has happened to you? We've all been crying our eyes out, and searching the house from top to bottom for you."

"Not quite from the top," thought Irene to herself, and she might have added, "not quite to the bottom," perhaps, if she had known all. But the one she would not, and the other she could not say.

"Oh, Lootie! I've had such a dreadful adventure!" she replied, and told her all about the cat with the long legs, and how she ran out upon the mountain, and came back again. But she said nothing of her grandmother or her lamp.

"And there we've been searching for you all over the house for more than an hour and a half!" exclaimed the nurse. "But that's no matter, now we've got you! Only, princess, I must say," she added, her mood changing, "what you ought to have done was to call for your own Lootie to come and help you, instead of running out of the house, and up the mountain, in that wild, I must say, foolish fashion."

"Well, Lootie," said Irene quietly, "perhaps if you had a big cat, all legs, running at you, you mightn't exactly know what was the wisest thing to do at the moment."

"I wouldn't run up the mountain, anyhow," returned Lootie.

"Not if you had time to think about it. But when those creatures came at you that night on the mountain, you were so frightened yourself that you lost your way home."

This put a stop to Lootie's reproaches. She had been on the point of saying that the long-legged cat must have been a twilight fancy of the princess's, but the memory of the horrors of that night, and of the talking-to which the king had given her in consequence, prevented her from saying what after all she did not half believe—having a strong suspicion that the cat was a goblin. For she knew nothing of the difference between the goblins and their creatures: she counted them all just goblins.

Without another word she went and got some fresh tea and bread and butter for the princess. Before she returned, the whole household, headed by the housekeeper, burst into the nursery to exult over their darling. The gentlemen-at-arms followed, and were ready enough to believe all she told them about the long-legged cat. Indeed, though wise enough to say nothing about it, they remembered, with no little horor, just such a creature amongst those they had surprised at their gambols upon the princess's lawn. In their own hearts they blamed themselves for not having kept better watch. And their captain gave orders that from this night the front door and all the windows on the ground floor should be locked immediately the sun set, and opened after upon no pretense whatever. The men-at-arms redoubled their vigilance, and for some time there was no further cause of alarm.

When the princess woke the next morning, her nurse was bending over her. "How your ring does glow this morning, princess! Just like a fiery rose!" she said.

"Does it, Lootie?" returned Irene. "Who gave me the ring, Lootie? I know I've had it a long time, but where did I get it? I don't remember."

"I think it must have been your mother gave it you, princess, but really, for as long as you have worn it. I don't remember that ever I heard," answered her nurse.

"I will ask my king-papa the next time he comes," said Irene.

Chapter 17

Springtime

*T*HE spring so dear to all creatures, young and old, came at last, and before the first few days of it had gone, the king rode through its budding valleys to see his little daughter. He had been in a distant part of his dominions all the winter, for he was not in the habit of stopping in one great city, or of visiting only his favorite country houses, but he moved from place to place, that all his people might know him. Wherever he journeyed, he kept a constant lookout for the ablest and best men to put into office, and wherever he found himself mistaken, and those he had appointed incapable or unjust, he removed them at once. Hence you see it was his care of the people that kept him from seeing his princess so often as he would have liked. You may wonder why he did not take her about with him; but there were several reasons against his doing so, and I suspect her great-great-grandmother had had a principal hand in preventing it. Once more Irene heard the bugle blast, and once more she was at the gate to meet her father as he rode up on his great white horse.

After they had been alone for a little while, she thought of what she had resolved to ask him.

"Please, King-papa," she said, "will you tell me where I got this pretty ring? I can't remember."

The king looked at it. A strange beautiful smile spread like sunshine over his face, and an answering smile, but at the same time a questioning one, spread like moonlight over Irene's.

"It was your queen-mama's once," he said.

"And why isn't it hers now?" asked Irene.

"She does not want it now," said the king, looking grave.

"Why doesn't she want it now?"

"Because she's gone where all those rings are made."

"And when shall I see her?" asked the princess.

"Not for some time yet," answered the king, and the tears came into his eyes.

Irene did not remember her mother and did not know why her father looked so, and why the tears came in his eyes; but she put her arms round his neck and kissed him, and asked no more questions.

The king was much disturbed on hearing the report of the gentlemen-at-arms concerning the creatures they had seen, and I presume would have taken Irene with him that very day, but for what the presence of the ring on her finger assured him of. About an hour before he left, Irene saw him go up the old stair, and he did not come down again till they were just ready to start; and she thought to herself that he had been up to see the old lady. When he went away he left other six gentlemen behind him, that there might be six of them always on guard.

And now, in the lovely spring weather, Irene was out on the mountain the greater part of the day. In the warmer hollows there were lovely primroses, and not so many that she ever got tired of them. As often as she saw a new one opening an eye of light in the blind earth, she would clap her hands with gladness, and unlike some children I know, instead of pulling it, would touch it as tenderly as if it had been a new baby, and, having made its acquaintance, would leave it as happy as she found it. She treated the plants on which they grew like birds' nests; every fresh flower was like a new little bird to her. She would pay visits to all the flower-nests she knew, remembering each by itself. She would go down on her hands and knees beside one and say, "Good morning! Are you all smelling very sweet this morning? Good-bye!" and then she would go to another nest, and say the same. It was a favorite amusement with her. There were many flowers up and down, and she loved them all, but the primroses were her favorites.

"They're not too shy, and they're not a bit forward," she would say to Lootie.

There were goats too about, over the mountain, and when the little kids came she was as pleased with them as with the flowers. The goats belonged to the miners mostly—a few of them to Curdie's mother; but there were a good many wild ones that seemed to belong to nobody. These the goblins counted theirs, and it was upon them partly that they lived. They set snares and dug pits for them, and did not scruple to take what tame ones happened to be caught; but they did not try to steal them in any other manner, because they were afraid of the dogs the hill people kept to watch them, for the knowing dogs always tried to bite their feet. But the goblins had a kind of sheep of their own—very queer creatures, which they drove out to feed at night, and the other goblin creatures were wise enough to keep good watch over them, for they knew they should have their bones by and by.

Chapter 18

Curdie's Clue

CURDIE was as watchful as ever, but was almost getting tired of his ill success. Every other night or so he followed the goblins about, as they went on digging and boring, and getting as near them as he could, watched them from behind stones and rocks; but as yet he seemed no nearer finding out what they had in view. As at first, he always kept hold of the end of his string, while his pickax, left just outside the hole by which he entered the goblins' country from the mine, continued to serve as an anchor and hold fast the other end. The goblins, hearing no more noise in that quarter, had ceased to apprehend an immediate invasion, and kept no watch.

One night, after dodging about and listening till he was nearly falling asleep with weariness, he began to roll up his ball, for he had resolved to go home to bed. It was not long, however, before he began to feel bewildered. One after another he passed goblin houses, caves, that is, occupied by goblin families, and at length was sure they were many more than he had passed as he came. He had to use great caution to pass unseen—they lay so close together. Could his string have led him wrong? He still followed winding it, and still it led him into more thickly populated quarters, until he became quite uneasy, and indeed apprehensive, for although he was not afraid of the cobs, he was afraid of not finding his way out. But what could he do? It was of no use to sit down and wait for the morning—the morning made no difference here. It was dark, and always dark, and if his string failed him he was helpless. He might even arrive within a yard of the mine and never know it. Seeing he could do nothing better, he would at least find where the end of his string was, and, if possible, how it had come to play him such a trick. He knew by the size of the ball that he was getting pretty near the last of it, when he began to feel a tugging and pulling at it. What could it mean?

Turning a sharp corner, he thought he heard strange sounds. These grew, as he went on, to a scuffling and growling and squeaking. And the noise increased, until, turning a second sharp corner, he found himself in the midst of it, and the same moment tumbled over a wallowing mass, which he knew must be a knot of the cobs' creatures. Before he could recover his feet, he had caught some great scratches on his face and several severe bites on his legs and arms. But as he scrambled to get up, his hand fell upon his pickax, and before the horrid beasts could do him any serious harm, he was laying about with it right and left in the dark. The hideous cries which followed gave him the satisfaction of knowing that he had punished some of them pretty smartly for their rudeness, and by their scampering and their retreating howls, he perceived that he had routed them. He stood for a little, weighing his battle-ax in his hand as if it had been the most precious lump of metal—but indeed no lump of gold itself could have been so precious at the time as that common tool—then untied the end of the string from it, put the ball in his pocket, and still stood thinking. It was clear that the cobs' creatures had found his ax, had between them carried it off, and had so led him he knew not where.

But for all his thinking he could not tell what he ought to do, until suddenly he became aware of a glimmer of light in the distance. Without a moment's hesitation he set out for it, as fast as the unknown and rugged way would permit. Yet again turning a corner, led by the dim light, he spied something quite new in his experience of the underground regions—a small irregular shape of something shining. Going up to it, he found it was a piece of mica, or Muscovy glass, called sheep-silver in Scotland, and the light flickered as if from a fire behind it. After trying in vain for some time to discover an entrance to the place where it was burning, he came at length to a small chamber in which an opening, high in the wall, revealed a glow beyond. To this opening he managed to scramble up, and then he saw a strange sight.

Below sat a little group of goblins around a fire, the smoke of which vanished in the darkness far aloft. The sides of the cave were full of shining minerals like those of the palace hall, and the company was evidently of a superior order, for everyone wore stones about head, or arms, or waist, shining dull gorgeous colors in the light of the fire. Nor had Curdie looked long before he recognized the king himself, and found that he had made his way into the inner apartment of the royal family. He had never had such a good chance of hearing something! He crept through the hole as softly as he could, scrambled a good way down the wall toward them without attracting attention, and then sat down and listened. The king, evidently the queen, and probably the crown prince and the prime minister were talking together. He was sure of the queen by her shoes, for as she warmed her feet at the fire, he saw them quite plainly.

"That *will* be fun!" said the one he took for the crown prince.

It was the first whole sentence he heard.

"I don't see why you should think it such a grand affair!" said his stepmother, tossing her head backward.

"You must remember, my spouse," interposed His Majesty, as if making excuse for his son, "he has got the same blood in him. His mother—"

"Don't talk to me of his mother! You positively encourage his unnatural fancies. Whatever belongs to *that* mother ought to be cut out of him."

"You forget yourself, my dear!" said the king.

"I don't," said the queen, "nor you either. If you expect *me* to approve of such coarse tastes, you will find yourself mistaken. *I* don't wear shoes for nothing."

"You must acknowledge, however," the king said, with a little groan, "that this at least is no whim of Harelip's, but a matter of state policy. You are well aware that his gratification comes purely from the pleasure of sacrificing himself to the public good. Does it not, Harelip?"

"Yes, Father, of course it does. Only it *will* be nice to make her cry. I'll have the skin taken off between her toes, and tie them up till they grow together. Then her feet will be like other people's, and there will be no occasion for her to wear shoes."

"Do you mean to insinuate *I*'ve got toes, you unnatural wretch?" cried the queen, and she moved angrily toward Harelip. The councillor, however, who was betwixt them, leaned forward so as to prevent her touching him, but only as if to address the prince.

"Your Royal Highness," he said, "possibly requires to be reminded that you have got three toes yourself—one on one foot, two on the other."

"Ha! Ha! Ha!" shouted the queen triumphantly.

The councillor, encouraged by this mark of favor, went on. "It seems to me, Your Royal Highness, it would greatly endear you to your future people, proving to them that you are not the less one of themselves that you had the misfortune to be born of a sun-mother, if you were to command upon yourself the comparatively slight operation which, in a more extended form, you so wisely meditate with regard to your future princess."

"Ha! Ha! Ha!" laughed the queen louder than before, and the king and the minister joined in the laugh. Harelip growled. and for a few moments the others continued to express their enjoyment of his discomfiture.

The queen was the only one Curdie could see with any distinctness. She sat sideways to him, and the light of the fire shone full upon her face. He could not consider her handsome. Her nose was certainly broader at the end than its extreme length, and her eyes, instead of being horizontal, were set up like two perpendicular eggs, one on the broad, the other on the small end. Her mouth was no bigger than a small buttonhole until she laughed, when it stretched from ear to ear—only to be sure, her ears were very nearly in the middle of her cheeks.

Anxious to hear everything they might say, Curdie ventured to slide down a smooth part of the rock just under him, to a projection below, upon which he thought to rest. But whether he was not careful enough, or the projection gave way, down he came with a rush on the floor of the cavern, bringing with him a great rumbling shower of stones.

The goblins jumped from their seats in more anger than consternation, for they had never yet seen anything to be afraid of in the palace. But when they saw Curdie with his pick in his hand their rage was mingled with fear, for they took him for the first of an invasion of miners. The king notwithstanding drew himself up to his full height of four feet, spread himself to his full breadth of three and a half, for he was the handsomest and squarest of all the goblins, and strutting up to Curdie, planted himself with outspread feet before him, and said with dignity, "Pray, what right have you in my palace?"

"The right of necessity, Your Majesty," answered Curdie. "I lost my way and did not know where I was wandering to."

"How did you get in?"

"By a hole in the mountain."

"But you are a miner! Look at your pickax!"

Curdie did look at it, answering, "I came upon it lying on the ground a little way from here. I tumbled over some wild beasts who were playing with it. Look, Your Majesty." And Curdie showed him how he was scratched and bitten.

The king was pleased to find him behave more politely than he had expected from what his people had told him concerning the miners, for he attributed it to the power of his own presence, but he did not therefore feel friendly to the intruder.

"You will oblige me by walking out of my dominions at once," he said, well knowing what a mockery lay in the words.

"With pleasure, if Your Majesty will give me a guide," said Curdie.

"I will give you a thousand," said the king with a scoffing air of magnificent liberality.

"One will be quite sufficient," said Curdie.

But the king uttered a strange shout, half halloo, half roar, and in rushed goblins till the cave was swarming. He said something to the first of them which Curdie could not hear, and it was passed from one to another till in a moment the farthest in the crowd had evidently heard and understood it. They began to gather about him in a way he did not relish, and he retreated toward the wall. They pressed upon him.

"Stand back," said Curdie, grasping his pickax tighter by his knee.

They only grinned and pressed closer. Curdie bethought himself and began to rhyme.

> Ten, twenty, thirty—
> You're all so very dirty!
> Twenty, thirty, forty—
> You're all so thick and snorty!"
>
> Thirty, forty, fifty—
> You're all so puff-and-snifty!
> Forty, fifty, sixty—
> Beast and man so mixty!
>
> Fifty, sixty, seventy—
> Mixty, maxty, leaventy!
> Sixty, seventy, eighty—
> All your cheeks so slaty!
>
> Seventy, eighty, ninety,
> All your hands so flinty!
> Eighty, ninety, hundred,
> Altogether dundred!

The goblins fell back a little when he began, and made horrible grimaces all through the rhyme, as if eating something so disagreeable that it set their teeth on edge and gave them the creeps. But whether it was that the rhyming words were most of them no words at all, for, a new rhyme being considered the more efficacious, Curdie had made it on the spur of the moment, or whether it was that the presence of the king and queen gave them courage, I cannot tell; but the moment the rhyme was over they crowded on him again, and out shot a hundred long arms, with a multitude of thick nailless fingers at the ends of them, to lay hold upon him. Then Curdie heaved up his ax. But being as gentle as courageous and not wishing to kill any of them, he turned the end which was square and blunt like a hammer, and with that came down a great blow on the head of the goblin nearest him. Hard as the heads of all goblins are, he thought he must feel that. And so he did, no doubt, but he only gave a horrible cry, and sprung at Curdie's throat. Curdie, however, drew back in time, and just at that critical moment remembered the vulnerable part of the goblin body. He made a sudden rush at the king and stamped with all his might on His Majesty's feet. The king gave a most unkingly howl and almost fell into the fire. Curdie then rushed into the crowd, stamping right and left.

The goblins drew back, howling on every side as he approached, but they were so crowded that few of those he attacked could escape his tread, and the shrieking and roaring that filled the cave would have appalled Curdie but for the good hope it gave him. They were tumbling over each other in heaps in their eagerness to rush from the cave, when a new assailant suddenly faced him—the queen, with flaming eyes and expanded nostrils, her hair standing half up from her head, rushed at him. She trusted in her shoes: they were of granite—hollowed like French sabots. Curdie would have endured much rather than hurt a woman, even if she was a goblin, but here was an affair of life and death: forgetting her shoes, he made a great stamp on one of her feet. But she instantly returned it with very different effect, causing him frightful pain, and almost disabling him. His only chance with her would have been to attack the granite shoes with his pickax, but before he could think of that she had caught him up in her arms and was rushing with him across the cave. She dashed him into a hole in the wall, with a force that almost stunned him. But although he could not move, he was not too far gone to hear her great cry, and the rush of multitudes of soft feet, followed by the sounds of something heaved up against the rock, after which came a multitudinous patter of stones falling near him. The last had not ceased when he grew very faint, for his head had been badly cut, and at last insensible.

When he came to himself there was perfect silence about him, and utter darkness, but for the merest glimmer in one tiny spot. He crawled to it, and found that they had heaved a slab against the mouth of the hole, past the edge of which a poor little gleam found its way from the fire. He could not move it a hairbreadth, for they had piled a great heap of stones against it. He crawled back to where he had been lying, in the faint hope of finding his pickax. But after a vain search he was at last compelled to acknowledge himself in an evil plight. He sat down and tried to think, but soon fell fast asleep.

Chapter 19

Goblin Counsels

*H*E must have slept a long time, for when he awoke he felt wonderfully restored—indeed almost well—and very hungry. There were voices in the outer cave.

Once more, then, it was night, for the goblins slept during the day and went about their affairs during the night.

In the universal and constant darkness of their dwelling they had no reason to prefer the one arrangement to the other, but from aversion to the sun-people they chose to be busy when there was least chance of their being met either by the miners below, when they were burrowing, or by the people of the mountain above, when they were feeding their sheep or catching their goats. And indeed it was only when the sun was away that the outside of the mountain was sufficiently like their own dismal regions to be endurable to their mole eyes, so thoroughly had they become unaccustomed to any light beyond that of their own fires and torches.

Curdie listened, and soon found that they were talking of himself.

"How long will it take?" asked Harelip.

"Not many days, I should think," answered the king. "They are poor feeble creatures, those sun-people, and want to be always eating. We can go a week at a time without food, and be all the better for it, but I've been told *they* eat two or three times every day! Can you believe it? They must be quite hollow inside—not at all like us, nine-tenths of whose bulk is solid flesh and bone. Yes—I judge a week of starvation will do for him."

"If *I* may be allowed a word," interposed the queen, "and I think I ought to have some voice in the matter—"

"The wretch is entirely at your disposal, my spouse," interrupted the king. "He is your property. You caught him yourself. We should never have done it."

The queen laughed. She seemed in far better humor than the night before.

"I was about to say," she resumed, "that it does seem a pity to waste so much fresh meat."

"What are you thinking of, my love?" said the king. "The very notion of starving him implies that we are not going to give him any meat, either salt or fresh."

"I'm not such a stupid as that comes to," returned Her Majesty. "What I mean is that by the time he is starved there will hardly be a picking upon his bones."

The king gave a great laugh.

"Well, my spouse, you may have him when you like," he said. "I don't fancy him for my part. I am pretty sure he is tough eating."

"That would be to honor instead of punish his insolence," returned the queen. "But why should our poor creatures be deprived of so much nourishment? Our little dogs and cats and pigs and small bears would enjoy him very much."

"You are the best of housekeepers, my lovely queen!" said her husband. "Let it be so by all means. Let us have our people in, and get him out and kill him at once. He deserves it. The mischief he might have brought upon us, now that he had penetrated so far as our most retired citadel, is incalculable. Or rather let us tie him hand and foot, and have the pleasure of seeing him torn to pieces by full torchlight in the great hall."

"Better and better!" cried the queen and the prince together, both of them clapping their hands. And the prince made an ugly noise with his harelip, just as if he had intended to be one at the feast.

"But," added the queen, bethinking herself, "he is so troublesome. For poor creatures as they are, there is something about those sun-people that is *very* troublesome. I cannot imagine how it is that with such superior strength and skill and understanding as ours, we permit them to exist at all. Why do we not destroy them entirely, and use their cattle and grazing lands at our pleasure? Of course, we don't want to live in their horrid country! It is far too glaring for our quieter and more refined tastes. But we might use it as a sort of outhouse, you know. Even our creatures' eyes might get used to it, and if they did grow blind that would be of no consequence, provided they grew fat as well. But we might even keep their great cows and other creatures, and then we should have a few more luxuries, such as cream and cheese, which at present we only taste occasionally, when our brave men have succeeded in carrying some off from their farms."

"It is worth thinking of," said the king, "and I don't know why *you* should be the first to suggest it, except that you have a positive genius for conquest. But still, as you say, there is something very troublesome about them, and it would be better, as I understand you to suggest, that we should starve him for a day or two first, so that he may be a little less frisky when we take him out."

> Once there was a goblin
> Living in a hole;
> Busy he was cobblin'
> A shoe without a sole.
>
> By came a birdie:
> "Goblin, what do you do?"
> "Cobble at a sturdie
> Upper leather shoe."
>
> "What's the good o' that, sir?"
> Said the little bird.
> "Why it's very pat, sir—
> Plain without a word.
>
> "Where 'tis all a hole, sir,
> Never can be holes:
> Why should their shoes have soles, sir,
> When they've got no souls?"

"What's that horrible noise?" cried the queen, shuddering from pot-metal head to granite shoes.

"I declare," said the king with solemn indignation, "it's the sun-creature in the hole!"

"Stop that disgusting noise!" cried the crown prince valiantly, getting up and standing in front of the heap of stones, with his face toward Curdie's prison. "Do now, or I'll break your head."

"Break away," shouted Curdie, and began singing again:

> Once there was a goblin,
> Living in a hole—

"I really cannot bear it," said the queen. "If I could only get at his horrid toes with my slippers again!"

"I think we had better go to bed," said the king.

"It's not time to go to bed," said the queen.

"I would if I was you," said Curdie.

"Impertinent wretch!" said the queen, with the utmost scorn in her voice.

"An impossible *if*," said His Majesty with dignity.

"Quite," returned Curdie, and began singing again:

> Go to bed,
> Goblin, do.
> Help the queen
> Take off her shoe.
>
> If you do,
> It will disclose
> A horrid set
> Of sprouting toes.

"What a lie!" roared the queen in a rage.

"By the way, that reminds me," said the king, "that for as long as we have been married, I have never seen your feet, queen. I think you might take off your shoes when you go to bed! They positively hurt me sometimes."

"I will do as I like," retorted the queen sulkily.

"You ought to do as your own hubby wishes you," said the king.

"I will not," said the queen.

"Then I insist upon it," said the king.

Apparently His Majesty approached the queen for the purpose of following the advice given by Curdie, for the latter heard a scuffle, and then a great roar from the king.

"Will you be quiet, then?" said the queen wickedly.

"Yes, yes, queen. I only meant to coax you."

"Hands off!" cried the queen triumphantly. "I'm going to

bed. You may come when you like. But as long as I am queen I will sleep in my shoes. It is my royal privilege. Harelip, go to bed."

"I'm going," said Harelip sleepily.

"So am I," said the king.

"Come along, then," said the queen, "and mind you are good, or I'll—"

"Oh, no, no, no!" screamed the king in the most supplicating of tones.

Curdie heard only a muttered reply in the distance, and then the cave was quite still.

They had left the fire burning, and the light came through brighter than before. Curdie thought it was time to try again if anything could be done. But he found he could not get even a finger through the chink between the slab and the rock. He gave a great rush with his shoulder against the slab, but it yielded no more than if it had been part of the rock. All he could do was to sit down and think again.

By and by he came to the resolution to pretend to be dying, in the hope they might take him out before his strength was too much exhausted to let him have a chance. Then, for the creatures, if he could but find his ax again, he would have no fear of them, and if it were not for the queen's horrid shoes, he would have no fear at all.

Meantime, until they should come again at night, there was nothing for him to do but forge new rhymes, now his only weapons. He had no intention of using them at present, of course, but it was well to have a stock, for he might live to want them, and the manufacture of them would help to while away the time.

Chapter 20

Irene's Clue

*T*HAT same morning early, the princess woke in a terrible fright. There was a hideous noise in her room—of creatures snarling and hissing and racketing about as if they were fighting. The moment she came to herself, she remembered something she had never thought of again—what her grandmother told her to do when she was frightened. She immediately took off her ring and put it under her pillow. As she did so she fancied she felt a finger and thumb take it gently from under her palm. "It must be my grandmother!" she said to herself, and the thought gave her such courage that she stopped to put on her dainty little slippers before running from the room. While doing this she caught sight of a long cloak of sky-blue, thrown over the back of a chair by the bedside. She had never seen it before, but it was evidently waiting for her. She put it on, and then, feeling with the forefinger of her right hand, soon found her grandmother's thread, which she proceeded at once to follow, expecting it would lead her straight up the old stair.

When she reached the door she found it went down and ran along the floor, so that she had almost to crawl in order to keep a hold of it. Then, to her surprise, and somewhat to her dismay, she found that instead of leading her toward the stair it turned in quite the opposite direction. It led her through certain narrow passages toward the kitchen, turning aside ere she reached it, and guiding her to a door which communicated with a small backyard. Some of the maids were already up, and this door was standing open. Across the yard the thread still ran along the ground, until it brought her to a door in the wall which opened upon the mountainside. When she had passed through, the thread rose to about half her height, and she could hold it with ease as she walked. It led her straight up the mountain.

The cause of her alarm was less frightful than she supposed. The cook's great black cat, pursued by the housekeeper's terrier, had bounced against her bedroom door, which had not been properly fastened, and the two had burst into the room together and commenced a battle royal. How the nurse came to sleep through it was a mystery, but I suspect the old lady had something to do with it.

It was a clear warm morning. The wind blew deliciously over the mountainside. Here and there she saw a late primrose, but she did not stop to call upon them. The sky was mottled with small clouds. The sun was not yet up, but some of their fluffy edges had caught his light, and hung out orange and gold-colored fringes upon the air. The dew lay in round drops upon the leaves, and hung like tiny diamond earrings from the blades of grass about her path.

"How lovely that bit of gossamer is!" thought the princess, looking at a long undulating line that shone at some distance from her up the hill. It was not the time for gossamers, though, and Irene soon discovered that it was her own thread, she saw shining on before her in the light of the morning. It was leading her she knew not whither, but she had never in her life been out before sunrise, and everything was so fresh and cool and lively and full of something coming, that she felt too happy to be afraid of anything.

After leading her up a good distance, the thread turned to the left, and down the path upon which she and Lootie had met Curdie. But she never thought of that, for now in the morning light, with its far outlook over the country, no path could have been more open and airy and cheerful. She could see the road almost to the horizon, along which she had so often watched her king-papa and his troop come shining, with the bugle blast cleaving the air before them, and it was like a companion to her. Down and down the path went, then up, and then down and then up again, getting rugged and more rugged as it went; and still along the path went the silvery thread, and still along the thread went Irene's little rosy-tipped forefinger.

By and by she came to a little stream that jabbered and prattled down the hill, and up the side of the stream went both path and thread. And still the path grew rougher and steeper, and the mountain grew wilder, till Irene began to think she was going a very long way from home; and when she turned to look back she saw that the level country had vanished and the rough bare mountain had closed in about her. But still on went the thread, and on went the princess. Everything around her was getting brighter and brighter as the sun came nearer, till at length his first rays all at once alighted on the top of a rock before her, like some golden creature fresh from the sky. Then she saw that the little stream ran out of a hole in that rock, that the path did not go past the rock, and that the thread was leading her straight up to it. A shudder ran through her from head to foot when she found that the thread was actually taking her into the hole out of which the stream ran. It ran out babbling joyously, but she had to go in.

She did not hesitate. Right into the hole she went, which was high enough to let her walk without stooping. For a little way there was a brown glimmer, but at the first turn it all but ceased, and before she had gone many paces she was in total darkness. Then she began to be frightened indeed. Every moment she kept feeling the thread backward and forward, and as she went farther and farther into the darkness of the great hollow mountain, she kept thinking more and more about her grandmother, and all that she had said to her, and how kind she had been, and how beautiful she was, and all about her lovely room, and the fire of roses, and the great lamp that sent its light through stone walls. And she became more and more sure that the thread could not have gone there of itself, and that her grandmother must have sent it.

But it tried her dreadfully when the path went down very steep, and especially when she came to places where she had to go down rough stairs, and even sometimes a ladder. Through one narrow passage after another, over lumps of rock and sand and clay, the thread guided her, until she came to a small hole through which she had to creep. Finding no change on the other side, "Shall I ever get back?" she thought, over and over again, wondering at herself that she was not ten times more frightened, and often feeling as if she were only walking in the story of a dream. Sometimes she heard the noise of water, a dull gurgling inside the rock. By and by she heard the sounds of blows, which came nearer and nearer, but again they grew duller, and almost died away. In a hundred directions she turned, obedient to the guiding thread.

At last she spied a dull red shine, and came up to the mica window, and thence away and round about, and right into a cavern, where glowed the red embers of a fire. Here the thread began to rise. It rose as high as her head and higher still. What *should* she do if she lost her hold? She was pulling it down! She might break it! She could see it far up, glowing as red as her fire opal in the light of the embers.

But presently she came to a huge heap of stones, piled in a slope against the wall of the cavern. On these she climbed, and soon recovered the level of the thread—only however to find, the next moment, that it vanished through the heap of stones, and left her standing on it, with her face to the solid rock. For one terrible moment she felt as if her grandmother had forsaken her. The thread which the spiders had spun far over the seas, which her grandmother had sat in the moonlight and spun again for her, which she had tempered in the rose fire and tied to her opal ring, had left her—had gone where she could no longer follow it—had brought her into a horrible cavern, and there left her! She was forsaken indeed!

"When *shall* I wake?" she said to herself in an agony, but the same moment knew that it was no dream. She threw herself upon the heap, and began to cry. It was well she did not know what creatures, one of them with stone shoes on her feet, were lying in the next cave. But neither did she know who was on the other side of the slab.

At length the thought struck her that at least she could follow the thread backward, and thus get out of the mountain, and home. She rose at once, and found the thread. But the instant she tried to feel it backward, it vanished from her touch.

Forward, it led her hand up to the heap of stones—backward it seemed nowhere. Neither could she see it as before in the light of the fire. She burst into a wailing cry, and again threw herself down on the stones.

Chapter 21

The Escape

*A*s the princess lay and sobbed she kept feeling the thread mechanically, following it with her finger many times up to the stones in which it disappeared. By and by she began, still mechanically, to poke her finger in after it between the stones as far as she could. All at once it came into her head that she might remove some of the stones and see where the thread went next. Almost laughing at herself for never having thought of this before, she jumped to her feet. Her fear vanished. Once more she was certain her grandmother's thread could not have brought her there just to leave her there, and she began to throw away the stones from the top as fast as she could, sometimes two or three at a handful, sometimes taking both hands to lift one. After clearing them away a little, she found that the thread turned and went straight downward. Hence, as the heap sloped a good deal, growing of course wider toward its base, she had to throw away a multitude of stones to follow the thread. But this was not all, for she soon found that the thread, after going straight down for a little way, turned

first sideways in one direction, then sideways in another, and
then shot, at various angles, hither and thither inside the heap,
so that she began to be afraid that to clear the thread she must
remove the whole huge gathering. She was dismayed at the
very idea, but, losing no time, set to work with a will; and with
aching back, and bleeding fingers and hands, she worked on,
sustained by the pleasure of seeing the heap slowly diminish and
begin to show itself on the opposite side of the fire. Another
thing which helped to keep up her courage was that, as often as
she uncovered a turn of the thread, instead of lying loose upon
the stones, it tightened up. This made her sure that her grandmother was at the end of it somewhere.

She had got about halfway down when she started, and
nearly fell with fright. Close to her ears as it seemed, a voice
broke out singing:

> Jabber, bother, smash!
> You'll have it all in a crash.
> Jabber, smash, bother!
> You'll have the worst of the pother.
> Smash, bother, jabber—

Here Curdie stopped, either because he could not find a
rhyme to *jabber,* or because he remembered what he had forgotten when he woke up at the sound of Irene's labors, that his
plan was to make the goblins think he was getting weak. But he
had uttered enough to let Irene know who he was.

"It's Curdie!" she cried joyfully.

"Hush! Hush!" came Curdie's voice again from somewhere.
"Speak softly."

"Why, you were singing loud!" said Irene.

"Yes. But they know I am here, and they don't know you
are. Who are you?"

"I'm Irene," answered the princess. "I know who you are quite well. You're Curdie."

"Why, how ever did you come here, Irene?"

"My great-great-grandmother sent me, and I think I've found out why. You can't get out, I suppose?"

"No, I can't. What are you doing?"

"Clearing away a huge heap of stones."

"There's a princess!" exclaimed Curdie, in a tone of delight, but still speaking in little more than a whisper. "I can't think how you got here, though."

"My grandmother sent me after her thread."

"I don't know what you mean," said Curdie, "but so you're there, it doesn't much matter."

"Oh, yes, it does!" returned Irene. "I should never have been here but for her."

"You can tell me all about it when we get out, then. There's no time to lose now," said Curdie.

And Irene went to work, as fresh as when she began.

"There's such a lot of stones!" she said. "It will take me a long time to get them all away."

"How far on have you got?" Asked Curdie.

"I've got about the half away, but the other half is ever so much bigger."

"I don't think you will have to move the lower half. Do you see a slab laid up against the wall?"

Irene looked, and felt about with her hands, and soon perceived the outlines of the slab.

"Yes," she answered, "I do."

"Then, I think," rejoined Curdie, "when you have cleared the slab about halfway down, or a little more, I shall be able to push it over."

"I must follow my thread," returned Irene, "whatever I do."

"What *do* you mean?" exclaimed Curdie

"You will see when you get out," answered the princess, and went on harder than ever.

But she was soon satisfied that what Curdie wanted done and what the thread wanted done were one and the same thing. For she saw not only that by following the turns of the thread she had been clearing the face of the slab, but that, a little more than halfway down, the thread went through the chink between the slab and the wall into the place where Curdie was confined, so that she could not follow it any farther until the slab was out of her way. As soon as she found this, she said in a right joyous whisper, "Now, Curdie! I think if you were to give a great push, the slab would tumble over."

"Stand quite clear of it, then," said Curdie, "and let me know when you are ready."

Irene got off the heap, and stood on one side of it.

"Now, Curdiè!" she cried.

Curdie gave a great rush with his shoulder against it. Out tumbled the slab on the heap, and out crept Curdie over the top of it.

"You've saved my life, Irene!" he whispered.

"Oh, Curdie! I'm so glad! Let's get out of this horrid place as fast as we can."

"That's easier said than done," returned he.

"Oh, no! It's quite easy," said Irene. "We have only to follow my thread. I am sure that it's going to take us out now."

She had already begun to follow it over the fallen slab into the hole, while Curdie was searching the floor of the cavern for his pickax.

"Here it is!" he cried. "No, it is not!" he added, in a

disappointed tone. "What can it be, then? I declare it's a torch. That *is* jolly! It's better almost than my pickax. Much better if it weren't for those stone shoes!" he went on as he lighted the torch by blowing the last embers of the expiring fire.

When he looked up, with the lighted torch casting a glare into the great darkness of the huge cavern, he caught sight of Irene disappearing in the hole out of which he had himself just come.

"Where are you going there?" he cried. "That's not the way out. That's where I couldn't get out."

"I know that," whispered Irene. "But this is the way my thread goes, and I must follow it."

"What nonsense that child talks!" said Curdie to himself. "I must follow her, though, and see that she comes to no harm. She will soon find she can't get out that way, and then she will come with me."

So he crept over the slab once more into the hole with his torch in his hand. But when he looked about in it, he could see her nowhere. And now he discovered that although the hole was narrow, it was much longer than he had supposed, for in one direction the roof came down very low, and the hole went off in a narrow passage, of which he could not see the end. The princess must have crept in there. He got on his knees and one hand, holding the torch with the other, and crept after her. The hole twisted about, in some parts so low that he could hardly get through, in others so high that he could not see the roof, but everywhere it was narrow—far too narrow for a goblin to get through, and so I presume they never thought that Curdie might. He was beginning to feel very uncomfortable lest something should have befallen the princess, when he heard her voice almost close to his ear, whispering, "Aren't you coming, Curdie?"

And when he turned the next corner, there she stood waiting for him.

"I knew you couldn't go wrong in that narrow hole, but now you must keep by me, for here is a great wide place," she said.

"I can't understand it," said Curdie, half to himself, half to Irene.

"Never mind," she returned. "Wait till we get out."

Curdie, utterly astonished that she had already got so far, and by a path he had known nothing of, thought it better to let her do as she pleased.

"At all events," he said again to himself, "I know nothing about the way, miner as I am; and she seems to think she does know something about it, though how she should passes my comprehension. So she's just as likely to find her way as I am, and as she insists on taking the lead, I must follow. We can't be much worse off than we are, anyhow."

Reasoning thus, he followed her a few steps, and came out in another great cavern, across which Irene walked in a straight line, as confidently as if she knew every step of the way. Curdie went on after her, flashing his torch about, and trying to see something of what lay around them. Suddenly he started back a pace as the light fell upon something close by which Irene was passing. It was a platform of rock raised a few feet from the floor and covered with sheepskins, upon which lay two horrible figures asleep, at once recognized by Curdie as the king and queen of the goblins. He lowered his torch instantly lest the light should awake them. As he did so it flashed upon his pickax, lying by the side of the queen, whose hand lay close by the handle of it.

"Stop one moment," he whispered. "Hold my torch, and don't let the light on their faces."

Irene shuddered when she saw the frightful creatures, whom she had passed without observing them, but she did as he requested, and turning her back, held the torch low in front of her. Curdie drew his pickax carefully away, and as he did so spied one of her feet, projecting from under the skins. The great clumsy granite shoe, exposed thus to his hand, was a temptation not to be resisted. He laid hold of it, and, with cautious efforts, drew it off. The moment he succeeded, he saw to his astonishment that what he had sung in ignorance, to annoy the queen, was actually true: She had six horrible toes. Overjoyed at his success, and seeing by the huge bump in the sheepskins where the other foot was, he proceeded to lift them gently, for, if he could only succeed in carrying away the other shoe as well, he would be no more afraid of the goblins than of so many flies. But as he pulled at the second shoe the queen gave a growl and sat up in bed. The same instant the king awoke also and sat up beside her.

"Run, Irene!" cried Curdie, for though he was not now in the least afraid for himself, he was for the princess.

Irene looked once round, saw the fearful creatures awake, and like the wise princess she was, dashed the torch on the ground and extinguished it, crying out, "Here, Curdie, take my hand."

He darted to her side, forgetting neither the queen's shoe nor his pickax, and caught hold of her hand as she sped fearlessly where her thread guided her. They heard the queen give a great bellow, but they had a good start, for it would be some time before they could get torches lighted to pursue them. Just as they thought they saw a gleam behind them, the thread brought them to a very narrow opening, through which Irene crept easily, and Curdie with difficulty.

"Now," said Curdie, "I think we shall be safe."

"Of course we shall," returned Irene.

"Why do you think so?" asked Curdie.

"Because my grandmother is taking care of us."

"That's all nonsense," said Curdie. "I don't know what you mean."

"Then if you don't know what I mean what right have you to call it nonsense?" asked the princess, a little offended.

"I beg your pardon, Irene," said Curdie, "I did not mean to vex you."

"Of course not," returned the princess. "But why do *you* think we shall be safe?"

"Because the king and queen are far too stout to get through that hole."

"There might be ways round," said the princess.

"To be sure there might; we are not out of it yet," acknowledged Curdie.

"But who do you mean by the king and queen?" asked the princess. "I should never call such creatures as those a king and a queen."

"Their own people do, though," answered Curdie.

The princess asked more questions, and Curdie, as they walked leisurely along, gave her a full account, not only of the character and habits of the goblins, so far as he knew them, but of his own adventures with them, beginning from the very night after that in which he had met her and Lootie upon the mountain. When he had finished, he begged Irene to tell him how it was that she had come to his rescue. So Irene, too, had to tell a long story, which she did in rather a roundabout manner, interrupted by many questions concerning things she had not explained. But her tale, as he did not believe more than half of it, left everything as unaccountable to him as before, and he was nearly as much perplexed as to what he must think of the princess. He could not believe that she was deliberately telling stories, and the only conclusion he could come to was that Lootie had been playing the child tricks, inventing no end of lies to frighten her for her own purposes.

"But how ever did Lootie come to let you go into the mountains alone?" he asked.

"Lootie knows nothing about it. I left her fast asleep—at least I think so. I hope my grandmother won't let her get into trouble, for it wasn't her fault at all, as my grandmother very well knows."

"But how *did* you find your way to me?" persisted Curdie.

"I told you already," answered Irene, "by keeping my finger upon my grandmother's thread, as I am doing now."

"You don't mean you've got the thread there?"

"Of course I do. I have told you so ten times already. I have hardly—except when I was removing the stones—taken my finger off it. There!" she added, guiding Curdie's hand to the thread, "you feel it yourself—don't you?"

"I feel nothing at all," replied Curdie.

"Then what *can* be the matter with your finger? *I* feel it perfectly. To be sure it is very thin, and in the sunlight looks just like the thread of a spider, though there are many of them twisted together to make it—but for all that I can't think why you shouldn't feel it as well as I do."

Curdie was too polite to say he did not believe there was any thread there at all. What he did say was, "Well, I can make nothing of it."

"I can, though, and you must be glad of that, for it will do for both of us."

"We're not out yet," said Curdie.

"We soon shall be," returned Irene confidently. And now the thread went downward, and led Irene's hand to a hole in the floor of the cavern, whence came a sound of running water which they had been hearing for some time.

"It goes into the ground now, Curdie," she said, stopping.

He had been listening to another sound, which is practiced ear had caught long ago, and which also had been growing louder. It was the noise the goblin miners made at their work, and they seemed to be at no great distance now. Irene heard it the moment she stopped.

"What is that noise?" she asked. "Do you know, Curdie?"

"Yes. It is the goblins digging and burrowing," he answered.

"And you don't know what they do it for?"

"No. I haven't the least idea. Would you like to see them?" he asked, wishing to have another try after their secret.

"If my thread took me there, I shouldn't much mind, but I don't want to see them, and I can't leave my thread. It leads me down into the hole, and we had better go at once."

"Very well. Shall I go in first?" said Curdie.

"No, better not. You can't feel the thread," she answered, stepping down through a narrow break in the floor of the cavern. "Oh!" she cried, "I am in the water. It is running strong—but it is not deep, and there is just room to walk. Make haste, Curdie."

He tried, but the hole was too small for him to get in.

"Go on a little bit," he said, shouldering his pickax.

In a few moments he had cleared a larger opening and followed her. They went on, down and down with the running water, Curdie getting more and more afraid it was leading them to some terrible gulf in the heart of the mountain. In one or two places he had to break away the rock to make room before even Irene could get through—at least without hurting herself. But at length they spied a glimmer of light, and in a minute more they were almost blinded by the full sunlight, into which they emerged. It was some little time before the princess could see well enough to discover that they stood in her own garden, close by the seat on which she and her king-papa had sat that afternoon. They had come out by the channel of the little stream. She danced and clapped her hands with delight.

"Now, Curdie!" she cried. "Won't you believe what I told you about my grandmother and her thread?"

For she had felt all the time that Curdie was not believing what she told him.

"There! Don't you see it shining on before us?" she added.

"I don't see anything," persisted Curdie.

"Then you must believe without seeing," said the princess, "for you can't deny it has brought us out of the mountain."

"I can't deny we *are* out of the mountain, and I should be very ungrateful indeed to deny that *you* had brought *me* out of it."

"I couldn't have done it but for the thread," persisted Irene.

"That's the part I don't understand."

"Well, come along, and Lootie will get you something to eat. I am sure you must want it very much."

"Indeed I do. But my father and mother will be so anxious about me, I must make haste—first up the mountain to tell my mother, and then down into the mine again to let my father know."

"Very well, Curdie, but you can't get out without coming

this way, and I will take you through the house, for that is nearest."

They met no one by the way, for, indeed, as before, the people were here and there and everywhere searching for the princess. When they got in Irene found that the thread, as she had half expected, went up the old staircase, and a new thought struck her. She turned to Curdie and said, "My grandmother wants me. Do come up with me and see her. Then you will know that I have been telling you the truth. Do come—to please me, Curdie. I can't bear you should think what I say is not true."

"I never doubted you believed what you said," returned Curdie. "I only thought you had some fancy in your head that was not correct."

"But do come, dear Curdie."

The little miner could not withstand this appeal, and though he felt shy in what seemed to him a huge grand house, he yielded, and followed her up the stair.

Chapter 22

The Old Lady and Curdie

*U*P the stair then they went, and the next and the next, and through the long rows of empty rooms, and up the little tower stair, Irene growing happier and happier as she ascended. There was no answer when she knocked at length at the door of the workroom, nor could she hear any sound of the spinning wheel, and once more her heart sank within her, but only for one moment, as she turned and knocked at the other door.

"Come in," answered the sweet voice of her grandmother, and Irene opened the door and entered, followed by Curdie.

"You darling!" cried the lady, who was seated by a fire of red roses mingled with white. "I've been waiting for you, and indeed getting a little anxious about you, and beginning to think whether I had not better go and fetch you myself."

As she spoke she took the little princess in her arms and placed her upon her lap. She was dressed in white now, and looking if possible more lovely than ever.

"I've brought Curdie, Grandmother. He wouldn't believe what I told him and so I've brought him."

"Yes—I see him. He is a good boy, Curdie, and a brave boy. Aren't you glad you've got him out?"

"Yes, Grandmother. But it wasn't very good of him not to believe me when I was telling him the truth."

"People must believe what they can, and those who believe more must not be hard upon those who believe less. I doubt if you would have believed it all yourself if you hadn't seen some of it."

"Ah, yes, Grandmother, I daresay! I'm sure you are right. But he'll believe now."

"I don't know that," replied her grandmother.

"Won't you, Curdie?" said Irene, looking round at him as she asked the question.

He was standing in the middle of the floor, staring, and looking strangely bewildered. This she thought came of his astonishment at the beauty of the lady.

"Make a bow to my grandmother, Curdie," she said.

"I don't see any grandmother," answered Curdie rather gruffly.

"Don't see my grandmother, when I'm sitting in her lap?" exclaimed the princess.

"No, I don't," reiterated Curdie, in an offended tone.

"Don't you see the lovely fire of roses—white ones amongst them this time?" asked Irene, almost as bewildered as he.

"No, I don't," answered Curdie, almost sulkily.

"Nor the blue bed? Nor the rose-colored counterpane? Nor the beautiful light, like the moon, hanging from the roof?"

"You're making game of me, Your Royal Highness, and after what we have come through together this day, I don't think it is kind of you," said Curdie, feeling very much hurt.

"Then what *do* you see?" asked Irene, who perceived at once that for her not to believe him was at least as bad as for him not to believe her.

"I see a big, bare, garret room—like the one in mother's cottage, only big enough to take the cottage itself in, and leave a good margin all round," answered Curdie.

"And what more do you see?"

"I see a tub, and a heap of musty straw, and a withered apple, and a ray of sunlight coming through a hole in the middle of the roof and shining on your head, and making all the place look a curious dusky brown. I think you had better drop it, princess, and go down to the nursery, like a good girl."

"But don't you hear my grandmother talking to me?" asked Irene, almost crying.

"No. I hear the cooing of a lot of pigeons. If you won't come down, I will go without you. I think that will be better anyhow, for I'm sure nobody who met us would believe a word we said to them. They would think we made it all up. I don't expect anybody but my own father and mother to believe me. They *know* I wouldn't tell a story."

"And yet *you* won't believe *me*, Curdie?" expostulated the princess, now fairly crying with vexation and sorrow at the gulf between her and Curdie.

"No. I *can't*, and I can't help it," said Curdie, turning to leave the room.

"What *shall* I do, Grandmother?" sobbed the princess, turning her face round upon the lady's bosom, and shaking with suppressed sobs.

"You must give him time," said her grandmother, "and you

must be content not to be believed for a while. It is very hard to bear, but I have had to bear it, and shall have to bear it many a time yet. I will take care of what Curdie thinks of you in the end. You must let him go now."

"You're not coming, are you?" asked Curdie.

"No, Curdie, my grandmother says I must let you go. Turn to the right when you get to the bottom of all the stairs, and that will take you to the hall where the great door is."

"Oh, I don't doubt I can find my way—without you, princess, or your old grannie's thread either!" said Curdie quite rudely.

"Oh, Curdie! Curdie!"

"I wish I had gone home at once. I'm very much obliged to you, Irene, for getting me out of that hole, but I wish you hadn't made a fool of me afterward."

He said this as he opened the door, which he left open, and, without another word, went down the stair. Irene listened with dismay to his departing footsteps.

Then turning again to the lady, "What does it all mean, Grandmother?" she sobbed, and burst into fresh tears.

"It means, my love, that I did not mean to show myself. Curdie is not yet able to believe some things. Seeing is not believing—it is only seeing. You remember I told you that if Lootie were to see me, she would rub her eyes, forget the half she saw, and call the other half nonsense."

"Yes, but I should have thought Curdie—"

"You are right. Curdie is much farther on than Lootie, and you will see what will come of it. But in the meantime you must be content, I say, to be misunderstood for a while. We are all very anxious to be understood, and it is very hard not to be. But there is one thing much more necessary."

"What is that, Grandmother?"

"To understand other people."

"Yes, Grandmother. I must be fair—for if I'm not fair to other people, I'm not worth being understood myself. I see. So as Curdie can't help it, I will not be vexed with him, but just wait."

"There's my own dear child," said her grandmother, and pressed her close to her bosom.

"Why weren't you in your workroom when we came up, Grandmother?" asked Irene, after a few moments' silence.

"If I had been there, Curdie would have seen me well enough. But why should I be there rather than in this beautiful room?"

"I thought you would be spinning."

"I've nobody to spin for just at present. I never spin without knowing for whom I am spinning."

"That reminds me—there is one thing that puzzles me," said the princess. "How are you to get the thread out of the mountain again? Surely you won't have to make another for *me*? That would be such a trouble!"

The lady set her down and rose and went to the fire. Putting in her hand, she drew it out again and held up the shining ball between her finger and thumb.

"I've got it now, you see," she said, coming back to the princess, "all ready for you when you want it."

Going to her cabinet, she laid it in the same drawer as before.

"And here is your ring," she added, taking it from the little finger of her left hand and putting it on the forefinger of Irene's right hand.

"Oh, thank you, Grandmother! I feel so safe now!"

"You are very tired my child," the lady went on. "Your hands are hurt with the stones, and I have counted nine bruises on you. Just look what you are like."

And she held up to her a little mirror which she had brought from the cabinet. The princess burst into a merry laugh at the sight. She was so draggled with the stream, and dirty with creeping through narrow places, that if she had seen the reflection without knowing it was a reflection, she would have taken herself for some gypsy child whose face was washed and hair combed about once in a month. The lady laughed too, and lifting her again upon her knee, took off her cloak and nightgown. Then she carried her to the side of the room. Irene wondered what she was going to do with her, but asked no questions—only starting a little when she found that she was going to lay her in the large silver bath, for as she looked into it, again she saw no bottom, but the stars shining miles away, as it seemed, in a great blue gulf. Her hands closed involuntarily on the beautiful arms that held her, and that was all.

The lady pressed her once more to her bosom, saying, "Do not be afraid, my child."

"No, Grandmother," answered the princess, with a little gasp, and the next instant she sank in the clear cool water.

When she opened her eyes, she saw nothing but a strange lovely blue over and beneath and all about her. The lady and the beautiful room had vanished from her sight, and she seemed utterly alone. But instead of being afraid, she felt more than happy—perfectly blissful. And from somewhere came the voice of the lady, singing a strange sweet song, of which she could distinguish every word, but of the sense she had only a feeling—no understanding. Nor could she remember a single line after it was gone. It vanished, like the poetry in a dream, as fast as it came. In after years, however, she would sometimes fancy that snatches of melody suddenly rising in her brain must be little phrases and fragments of the air of that song, and the very fancy would make her happier, and abler to do her duty.

How long she lay in the water she did not know. It seemed a long time—not from weariness but from pleasure. But at last she felt the beautiful hands lay hold of her, and through the gurgling water she was lifted out into the lovely room. The lady carried her to the fire, and sat down with her in her lap, and dried her tenderly with the softest towel. It was so different from Lootie's drying. When the lady had done, she stooped to the fire, and drew from it her nightgown, as white as snow.

"How delicious!" exclaimed the princess. "It smells of all the roses in the world, I think."

When she stood up on the floor she felt as if she had been made over again. Every bruise and all weariness were gone, and her hands were soft and whole as ever.

"Now I am going to put you to bed for a good sleep," said her grandmother.

"But what will Lootie be thinking? And what am I to say to her when she asks me where I have been?"

"Don't trouble yourself about it. You will find it all come right," said her grandmother, and laid her into the blue bed, under the rosy counterpane.

"There is just one thing more," said Irene. "I am a little anxious about Curdie. As I brought him into the house, I ought to have seen him safe on his way home."

"I took care of all that," answered the lady. "I told you to let him go, and therefore I was bound to look after him. Nobody saw him, and he is now eating a good dinner in his mother's cottage far up in the mountain."

"Then I will go to sleep," said Irene, and in a few minutes she was fast asleep.

Chapter 23

Curdie and His Mother

CURDIE went up the mountain neither whistling nor singing, for he was vexed with Irene for taking him in, as he called it, and he was vexed with himself for having spoken to her so angrily. His mother gave a cry of joy when she saw him, and at once set about getting him something to eat, asking him questions all the time, which he did not answer so cheerfully as usual. When his meal was ready, she left him to eat it, and hurried to the mine to let his father know he was safe. When she came back, she found him fast asleep upon her bed; nor did he wake until his father came home in the evening.

"Now, Curdie," his mother said, as they sat at supper, "tell us the whole story from beginning to end, just as it all happened."

Curdie obeyed, and told everything to the point where they came out upon the lawn in the garden of the king's house.

"And what happened after that?" asked his mother. "You haven't told us all. You ought to be very happy at having got away from those demons, and instead of that I never saw you so gloomy. There must be something more. Besides, you do not speak of that lovely child as I should like to hear you. She saved your life at the risk of her own, and yet somehow you don't seem to think much of it."

"She talked such nonsense!" answered Curdie, "and told me a pack of things that weren't a bit true, and I can't get over it."

"What were they?" asked his father. "Your mother may be able to throw some light upon them."

Then Curdie made a clean breast of it, and told them everything.

They all sat silent for some time, pondering the strange tale. At last Curdie's mother spoke.

"You confess, my boy," she said, "there is something about the whole affair, you do not understand?"

"Yes, of course, Mother," he answered. "I cannot understand how a child knowing nothing about the mountain, or even that I was shut up in it, should come all that way alone, straight to where I was, and then, after getting me out of the hole, lead me out of the mountain too, where I should not have known a step of the way if it had been as light as in the open air."

"Then you have no right to say what she told you was not true. She did take you out, and she must have had something to guide her: why not a thread as well as a rope, or anything else? There is something you cannot explain, and her explanation may be the right one."

"It's no explanation at all, Mother, and I can't believe it."

"That may be only because you do not understand it. If you did, you would probably find it was an explanation, and believe it thoroughly. I don't blame you for not being able to believe it, but I do blame you for fancying such a child would try to deceive you. Why should she? Depend upon it, she told you all she knew. Until you had found a better way of accounting for it all, you might at least have been more sparing of your judgment."

"That is what something inside me has been saying all the time," said Curdie, hanging down his head. "But what do you make of the grandmother? That is what I can't get over. To take me up to an old garret, and try to persuade me against the sight of my own eyes that it was a beautiful room, with blue walls and silver stars, and no end of things in it, when there was nothing there but an old tub and a withered apple and a heap of straw and a sunbeam! It was too bad! She *might* have had some old woman there at least to pass for her precious grandmother!"

"Didn't she speak as if she saw those other things herself, Curdie?"

"Yes. That's what bothers me. You would have thought she really meant and believed that she saw every one of the things she talked about. And not one of them there! It was too bad, I say."

"Perhaps some people can see things other people can't see, Curdie," said his mother very gravely. "I think I will tell you something I saw myself once—only perhaps you won't believe me either!"

"Oh, Mother, Mother!" cried Curdie, bursting into tears, "I don't deserve that, surely!"

"But what I am going to tell you is very strange," persisted his mother, "and if having heard it you were to say I must have been dreaming, I don't know that I should have any right to be vexed with you, though I know at least that I was not asleep."

"Do tell me, Mother. Perhaps it will help me to think better of the princess."

"That's why I am tempted tell you," replied his mother.

"But first, I may as well mention that, according to old whispers, there is something more than common about the king's family; and the queen was of the same blood, for they were cousins of some degree. There were strange stories told concerning them—all good stories—but strange, very strange. What they were I cannot tell, for I only remember the faces of my grandmother and my mother as they talked together about them. There was wonder and awe—not fear—in their eyes, and they whispered, and never spoke aloud. But what I saw myself was this: Your father was going to work in the mine one night, and I had been down with his supper. It was soon after we were married, and not very long before you were born. He came with me to the mouth of the mine, and left me to go home alone, for I knew the way almost as well as the floor of our own cottage. It was pretty dark, and in some parts of the road where the rocks overhung nearly quite dark. But I got along perfectly well, never thinking of being afraid, until I reached a spot you know well enough, Curdie, where the path has to make a sharp turn out of the way of a great rock on the left-hand side. When I got there, I was suddenly surrounded by about half a dozen of the cobs, the first I had ever seen, although I had heard tell of them often enough. One of them blocked up the path, and they all began tormenting and teasing me in a way it makes me shudder to think of even now."

"If I had only been with you!" cried father and son in a breath.

The mother gave a funny little smile, and went on.

"They had some of their horrible creatures with them too, and I must confess I was dreadfully frightened. They had torn my clothes very much, and I was afraid they were going to tear myself to pieces, when suddenly a great white soft light shone upon me. I looked up. A broad ray, like a shining road, came down from a large globe of silvery light, not very high up, indeed not quite so high as the horizon—so it could not have been a new star or another moon or anything of that sort. The cobs dropped persecuting me, and looked dazed, and I thought they were going to run away, but presently they began again. The same moment, however, down the path from the globe of light came a bird, shining like silver in the sun. It gave a few rapid flaps first, and then, with its wings straight out, shot sliding down the slope of the light. It looked to me just like a white pigeon. But whatever it was, when the cobs caught sight of it coming straight down upon them, they took to their heels and scampered away across the mountain, leaving me safe, only much frightened. As soon as it had sent them off, the bird went gliding again up the light, and the moment it reached the globe the light disappeared, just as if a shutter had been closed over a window, and I saw it no more. But I had no more trouble with the cobs that night or ever after."

"How strange!" exclaimed Curdie.

"Yes, it was strange, but I can't help believing it, whether you do or not," said his mother.

"It's exactly as your mother told it to me the very next morning," said his father.

"You don't think I'm doubting my own mother?" cried Curdie.

"There are other people in the world quite as well worth believing as your own mother," said his mother. "I don't know that she's so much the fitter to be believed that she happens to be *your* mother, Mr. Curdie. There are mothers far more likely to tell lies than the little girl I saw talking to the primroses a few weeks ago. If she were to lie I should begin to doubt my own word."

"But princesses *have* told lies as well as other people," said Curdie.

"Yes, but not princesses like that child. She's a good girl, I am certain, and that's more than being a princess. Depend upon it, you will have to be sorry for behaving so to her, Curdie. You ought at least to have held your tongue."

"I am sorry now," answered Curdie.

"You ought to go and tell her so, then."

"I don't see how I could manage that. They wouldn't let a miner-boy like me have a word with her alone, and I couldn't tell her before that nurse of hers. She'd be asking ever so many questions, and I don't know how many the little princess would like me to answer. She told me that Lootie didn't know anything about her coming to get me out of the mountain. I am certain she would have prevented her somehow if she had known it. But I may have a chance before long, and meantime I must try to do something for her. I think, Father, I have got on the track at last."

"Have you, indeed, my boy?" said Peter. "I am sure you deserve some success; you have worked very hard for it. What have you found out?"

"It's difficult, you know, Father, inside the mountain, especially in the dark, and not knowing what turns you have taken, to tell the lie of things outside."

"Impossible, my boy, without a chart, or at least a compass," returned his father.

"Well, I think I have nearly discovered in what direction the cobs are mining. If I am right, I know something else that I can put to it, and then one and one will make three."

"They very often do, Curdie, as we miners ought to be very

well aware. Now tell us, my boy, what the two things are, and see whether we can guess at the same third as you."

"I don't see what that has to do with the princess," interposed his mother.

"I will soon let you see that, Mother. Perhaps you may think me foolish, but until I am sure there is nothing in my present fancy, I am more determined than ever to go on with my observations. Just as we came to the channel by which we got out, I heard the miners at work somewhere near—I think down below us. Now since I began to watch them, they have mined a good half mile, in a straight line, and so far as I am aware, they are working in no other part of the mountain. But I never could tell in what direction they were going. When we came out in the king's garden, however, I thought at once whether it was possible they were working toward the king's house; and what I want to do tonight is to make sure whether they are or not. I will take a light with me—"

"Oh, Curdie," cried his mother, "then they will see you."

"I'm no more afraid of them now than I was before," rejoined Curdie, "now that I've got this precious shoe. They can't make another such in a hurry, and one bare foot will do for my purpose. Woman as she may be, I won't spare her next time. But I shall be careful with my light, for I don't want them to see me. I won't stick it in my hat."

"Go on, then, and tell us what you mean to do."

"I mean to take a bit of paper with me and a pencil, and go in at the mouth of the stream by which we came out. I shall mark on the paper as near as I can the angle of every turning I take until I find the cobs at work, and so get a good idea in what direction they are going. If it should prove to be nearly parallel with the stream, I shall know it is toward the king's house they are working."

"And what if you should? How much wiser will you be then?"

"Wait a minute, Mother dear. I told you that when I came upon the royal family in the cave, they were talking of their prince—Harelip, they called him—marrying a sun-woman—that means one of us—one with toes to her feet. Now in the speech one of them made that night at their great gathering, of which I heard only a part, he said that peace would be secured for a generation at least by the pledge the prince would hold for the good behavior of *her* relatives: that's what he said, and he must have meant the sun-woman the prince was to marry. I am quite sure the king is much too proud to wish his son to marry any but a princess, and much too knowing to fancy that his having a peasant woman for a wife would be of any great advantage to them."

"I see what you are driving at now," said his mother.

"But," said his father, "our king would dig the mountain to the plain before he would have his princess the wife of a cob, if he were ten times a prince."

"Yes, but they think so much of themselves!" said his mother. "Small creatures always do. The bantam is the proudest cock in my little yard."

"And I fancy," said Curdie, "if they once got her, they would tell the king they would kill her except he consented to the marriage."

"They might say so," said his father, "but they wouldn't kill her, they would keep her alive for the sake of the hold it gave them over our king. Whatever he did to them, they would threaten to do the same to the princess."

"And they are bad enough to torment her just for their own amusement—I know that," said his mother.

"Anyhow, I will keep a watch on them, and see what they are up to," said Curdie. "It's too horrible to think of. I daren't let myself do it. But they shan't have her—at least if I can help it. So, mother dear—my clue is all right—will you get me a bit of paper and a pencil and a lump of pease pudding, and I will set out at once. I saw a place where I can climb over the wall of the garden quite easily."

"You must mind and keep out of the way of the men on the watch," said his mother.

"That I will. I don't want them to know anything about it. They would spoil it all. The cobs would only try some other plan— they are such obstinate creatures! I shall take good care, Mother. They won't kill and eat me, either, if they should come upon me. So you needn't mind them."

His mother got him what he had asked for, and Curdie set out. Close beside the door by which the princess left the garden for the mountain stood a great rock, and by climbing it Curdie got over the wall. He tied his clue to a stone just inside the channel of the stream, and took his pickax with him. He had not gone far before he encountered a horrid creature coming toward the mouth. The spot was too narrow for two of almost any size or shape, and besides Curdie had no wish to let the creature pass. Not being able to use his pickax, however, he had a severe struggle with him, and it was only after receiving many bites, some of them bad, that he succeeded in killing him with his pocketknife. Having dragged him out, he made haste to get in again before another should stop up the way.

I need not follow him farther in this night's adventures. He returned to his breakfast, satisfied that the goblins were mining in the direction of the palace—on so low a level that their intention must, he thought, be to burrow under the walls of the king's house, and rise up inside it—in order, he fully believed, to lay hands on the little princess, and carry her off for a wife to their horrid Harelip.

Chapter 24

Irene Behaves
Like a Princess

WHEN the princess awoke from the sweetest
of sleeps, she found her nurse bending over her, the housekeeper looking over the nurse's shoulder, and the laundry maid
looking over the housekeeper's. The room was full of women
servants, and the gentlemen-at-arms, with a long column of
servants behind them, were peeping or trying to peep in at the
door of the nursery.

"Are those horrid creatures gone?" asked the princess, remembering first what had terrified her in the morning.

"You naughty, naughty little princess!" cried Lootie.

Her face was very pale, with red streaks in it, and she looked
as if she were going to shake her, but Irene said nothing—only
waited to hear what should come next.

"How *could* you get under the clothes like that, and make us
all fancy you were lost! And keep it up all day too! You *are* the
most obstinate child! It's anything but fun to us, I can tell you!"

It was the only way the nurse could account for her disappearance.

"I didn't do that, Lootie," said Irene, very quietly.

"Don't tell stories!" cried her nurse quite rudely.

"I shall tell you nothing at all," said Irene.

"That's just as bad," said the nurse.

"Just as bad to say nothing at all as to tell stories?" exclaimed the princess. "I will ask my papa about that. He won't say so. And I don't think he will like you to say so."

"Tell me directly what you mean by it!" screamed the nurse, half wild with anger at the princess, and fright at the possible consequences to herself.

"When I tell you the truth, Lootie," said the princess, who somehow did not feel at all angry, "you say to me 'Don't tell stories.' It seems I must tell stories before you will believe me."

"You are very rude, princess," said the nurse.

"You are so rude, Lootie, that I will not speak to you again till you are sorry. Why should I, when I know you will not believe me?" returned the princess.

For she did know perfectly well that if she were to tell Lootie what she had been about, the more she went on to tell her, the less would she believe her.

"You are the most provoking child!" cried her nurse. "You deserve to be well punished for your wicked behavior."

"Please, Mrs. Housekeeper," said the princess, "will you take me to your room, and keep me till my king-papa comes? I will ask him to come as soon as he can."

Everyone stared at these words. Up to this moment they had all regarded her as little more than a baby.

But the housekeeper was afraid of the nurse, and sought to

patch matters up, saying, "I am sure, princess, nursie did not mean to be rude to you."

"I do not think my papa would wish me to have a nurse who spoke to me as Lootie does. If she thinks I tell lies, she had better either say so to my papa, or go away. Sir Walter, will you take charge of me?"

"With the greatest of pleasure, princess," answered the captain of the gentlemen-at-arms, walking with his great stride into the room. The crowd of servants made eager way for him, and he bowed low before the little princess's bed. "I shall send my servant at once, on the fastest horse in the stable, to tell your king-papa that Your Royal Highness desires his presence. When you have chosen one of these underservants to wait upon you, I shall order the room to be cleared."

"Thank you very much, Sir Walter," said the princess, and her eyes glanced toward a rosy-cheeked girl who had lately come to the house as a scullery maid.

But when Lootie saw the eyes of her dear princess going in search of another instead of her, she fell upon her knees by the bedside, and burst into a great cry of distress.

"I think, Sir Walter," said the princess, "I will keep Lootie. But I put myself under your care, and you need not trouble my king-papa until I speak to you again. Will you all please to go away? I am quite safe and well, and I did not hide myself for the sake either of amusing myself, or of troubling my people. Lootie, will you please to dress me."

Chapter 25

Curdie Comes to Grief

*E*VERYTHING was for some time quiet above-ground. The king was still away in a distant part of his dominions. The men-at-arms kept watching about the house. They had been considerably astonished by finding at the foot of the rock in the garden the hideous body of the goblin creature killed by Curdie, but they came to the conclusion that it had been slain in the mines and had crept out there to die; and except an occasional glimpse of a live one they saw nothing to cause alarm. Curdie kept watching in the mountain, and the goblins kept burrowing deeper into the earth. As long as they went deeper, there was, Curdie judged, no immediate danger.

To Irene the summer was as full of pleasure as ever, and for a long time, although she often thought of her grandmother during the day, and often dreamed about her at night, she did not see her. The kids and the flowers were as much her delight as ever, and she made as much friendship with the miners' children she met on the mountain as Lootie would permit; but Lootie had very foolish notions concerning the dignity of a princess, not understanding that the truest princess is just the one who loves all her brothers and sisters best, and who is most able to do them good by being humble toward them. At the same time she was considerably altered for the better in her behavior to the princess. She could not help seeing that she was no longer a mere child, but wiser than her age would account for. She kept foolishly whispering to the servants, however—sometimes that the princess was not right in her mind, sometimes that she was too good to live, and other nonsense of the same sort.

All this time Curdie had to be sorry, without a chance of confessing, that he had behaved so unkindly to the princess. This perhaps made him the more diligent in his endeavors to serve her. His mother and he often talked on the subject, and she comforted him, and told him she was sure he would someday have the opportunity he so much desired.

Here I should like to remark, for the sake of princes and princesses in general, that it is a low and contemptible thing to refuse to confess a fault, or even an error. If a true princess has done wrong, she is always uneasy until she has had an opportunity of throwing the wrongness away from her by saying, "I did it, and I wish I had not, and I am sorry for having done it." So you see there is some ground for supposing that Curdie was not a miner only, but a prince as well. Many such instances have been known in the world's history.

At length, however, he began to see signs of a change in the proceedings of the goblin excavators: they were going no deeper but had commenced running on a level, and he watched them, therefore, more closely than ever. All at once, one night, coming to a slope of very hard rock, they began to ascend along the inclined plane of its surface. Having reached the top, they

went again on a level for a night or two, after which they began
to ascend once more, and kept on at a pretty steep angle. At
length Curdie judged it time to transfer his observation to
another quarter, and the next night he did not go to the mine
at all, but, leaving his pickax and clue at home, and taking
only his usual lumps of bread and pease pudding, went down
the mountain to the king's house. He climbed over the wall,
and remained in the garden the whole night, creeping on hands
and knees from one spot to the other, and lying at full length
with his ear to the ground, listening. But he heard nothing
except the tread of the men-at-arms as they marched about,
whose observation, as the night was cloudy and there was no
moon, he had little difficulty in avoiding. For several following
nights he continued to haunt the garden and listen, but with
no success.

At length, early one evening, whether it was that he had got
careless of his own safety, or that the growing moon had
become strong enough to expose him, his watching came to a
sudden end. He was creeping from behind the rock where the
stream ran out, for he had been listening all round it in the
hope it might convey to his ear some indication of the where-
abouts of the goblin miners, when just as he came into the
moonlight on the lawn, a whizz in his ear and a blow upon his
leg startled him. He instantly squatted in the hope of eluding
further notice. But when he heard the sound of running feet,
he jumped up to take the chance of escape by flight. He fell,
however, with a keen shoot of pain, for the bolt of a crossbow
had wounded his leg, and the blood was now streaming from it.
He was instantly laid hold of by two or three of the men-at-
arms. It was useless to struggle, and he submitted in silence.

"It's a boy!" cried several of them together, in a tone of amazement. "I thought it was one of those demons."

"What are you about here?"

"Going to have a little rough usage, apparently," said Curdie, laughing, as the men shook him.

"Impertinence will do you no good. You have no business here in the king's grounds, and if you don't give a true account of yourself, you shall fare as a thief."

"Why, what else could he be?" said one.

"He might have been after a lost kid, you know," suggested another.

"I see no good in trying to excuse him. He has no business here, anyhow."

"Let me go away, then, if you please," said Curdie.

"But we don't please—not except you give a good account of yourself."

"I don't feel quite sure whether I can trust you," said Curdie.

"We are the king's own men-at-arms," said the captain courteously, for he was taken with Curdie's appearance and courage.

"Well, I will tell you all about it—if you will promise to listen to me and not do anything rash."

"I call that cool!" said one of the party, laughing. "He will tell us what mischief he was about, if we promise to do as pleases him."

"I was about no mischief," said Curdie.

But ere he could say more he turned faint, and fell senseless on the grass. Then first they discovered that the bolt they had shot, taking him for one of the goblin creatures, had wounded him.

They carried him into the house and laid him down in the hall. The report spread that they had caught a robber, and the servants crowded in to see the villain. Amongst the rest came the nurse. The moment she saw him she exclaimed with indignation, "I declare it's the same young rascal of a miner that was rude to me and the princess on the mountain. He actually wanted to kiss the princess. *I* took good care of that—the wretch! And *he* was prowling about—was he? Just like his impudence!"

The princess being fast asleep, she could misrepresent at her pleasure.

When he heard this, the captain, although he had considerable doubt of its truth, resolved to keep Curdie a prisoner until they could search into the affair. So, after they had brought him round a little, and attended to his wound, which was rather a bad one, they laid him, still exhausted from the loss of blood, upon a mattress in a disused room—one of those already so often mentioned—and locked the door, and left him. He passed a troubled night, and in the morning they found him talking wildly. In the evening he came to himself, but felt very weak, and his leg was exceedingly painful. Wondering where he was, and seeing one of the men-at-arms in the room, he began to question him, and soon recalled the events of the preceding night. As he was himself unable to watch any more, he told the soldier all he knew about the goblins, and begged him to tell his companions, and stir them up to watch with tenfold vigilance. But whether it was that he did not talk quite coherently, or that the whole thing appeared incredible, certainly the man concluded that Curdie was only raving still, and tried to coax him into holding his tongue.

This, of course, annoyed Curdie dreadfully, who now felt in his turn what it was not to be believed, and the consequence was that his fever returned, and by the time when, at his persistent entreaties, the captain was called, there could be no doubt that he was raving. They did for him what they could, and promised everything he wanted, but with no intention of fulfillment. At last he went to sleep, and when at length his sleep grew profound and peaceful, they left him, locked the door again, and withdrew, intending to revisit him early in the morning.

Chapter 26

The Goblin Miners

*T*HAT same night several of the servants were having a chat together before going to bed. "What can that noise be?" said one of the housemaids, who had been listening for a moment or two.

"I've heard it the last two nights," said the cook. "If there were any about the place, I should have taken it for rats, but my Tom keeps them far enough."

"I've heard, though," said the scullery maid, "that rats move about in great companies sometimes. There may be an army of them invading us. I've heard the noises yesterday and today too."

"It'll be grand fun, then, for my Tom and Mrs. Housekeeper's Bob," said the cook. "They'll be friends for once in their lives, and fight on the same side. I'll engage Tom and Bob together will put to flight any number of rats."

"It seems to me," said the nurse, "that the noises are much too loud for that. I have heard them all day, and my princess has asked me several times what they could be. Sometimes they sound like distant thunder, and sometimes like the noises you hear in the mountain from those horrid miners underneath."

"I shouldn't wonder," said the cook, "if it was the miners after all. They may have come on some hole in the mountain through which the noises reach to us. They are always boring and blasting and breaking, you know."

As she spoke there came a great rolling rumble beneath them, and the house quivered. They all started up in affright and rushing to the hall found the gentlemen-at-arms in consternation also. They had sent to wake their captain—who said from their description that it must have been an earthquake, an occurrence which, although very rare in that country, had taken place almost within the century—and then went to bed again, strange to say, and fell fast asleep without once thinking of Curdie, or associating the noises they had heard with what he had told them. He had not believed Curdie. If he had, he would at once have thought of what he had said, and would have taken precautions. As they heard nothing more, they concluded that Sir Walter was right, and that the danger was over for perhaps another hundred years.

The fact, as discovered afterward, was that the goblins had, in working up a second sloping face of stone, arrived at a huge block which lay under the cellars of the house, within the line of the foundations. It was so round that when they succeeded, after hard work, in dislodging it without blasting, it rolled thundering down the slope with a bounding, jarring roll, which shook the foundations of the house. The goblins were themselves dismayed at the noise, for they knew, by careful spying and measuring, that they must now be very near, if not under the king's house, and they feared giving an alarm. They therefore remained quiet for a while, and when they began to work again, they no doubt thought themselves very fortunate in coming upon a vein of sand which filled a winding fissure in the rock on which the house was built. By scooping this away they came out in the king's wine cellar.

No sooner did they find where they were, than they scurried back again, like rats into their holes, and running at full speed to the goblin palace, announced their success to the king and queen with shouts of triumph. In a moment the goblin royal family and the whole goblin people were on their way in hot haste to the king's house, each eager to have a share in the glory of carrying off that same night the Princess Irene.

The queen went stumping along in one shoe of stone and one of skin. This could not have been pleasant, and my readers may wonder that, with such skillful workmen about her, she had not yet replaced the shoe carried off by Curdie. As the king, however, had more than one ground of objection to her stone shoes, he no doubt took advantage of the discovery of her toes and threatened to expose her deformity if she had another made. I presume he insisted on her being content with skin shoes, and allowed her to wear the remaining granite one on the present occasion only because she was going out to war.

They soon arrived in the king's wine cellar, and regardless of its huge vessels, of which they did not know the use, proceeded at once, but as quietly as they could, to force the door that led upward.

Chapter 27

The Goblins in the King's House

WHEN Curdie fell asleep he began at once to dream. He thought he was ascending the mountainside from the mouth of the mine, whistling and singing "Ring, dod, bang!" when he came upon a woman and child who had lost their way; and from that point he went on dreaming everything that had happened to him since he thus met the princess and Lootie: how he had watched the goblins, how he had been taken by them, how he had been rescued by the princess, everything, indeed, until he was wounded, captured, and imprisoned by the men-at-arms. And now he thought he was lying wide awake where they had laid him, when suddenly he heard a great thundering sound.

"The cobs are coming!" he said. "They didn't believe a word I told them! The cobs'll be carrying off the princess from under their stupid noses! But they shan't! That they shan't!"

He jumped up, as he thought, and began to dress, but, to his dismay, found that he was still lying in bed.

"Now then, I will!" he said. "Here goes! I *am* up now!"

But yet again he found himself snug in bed. Twenty times he tried, and twenty times he failed, for in fact he was not awake, only dreaming that he was. At length in an agony of despair, fancying he heard the goblins all over the house, he gave a great cry. Then there came, as he thought, a hand upon the lock of his door. It opened, and, looking up, he saw a lady with white hair, carrying a silver box in her hand, enter the room. She came to his bed, he thought, stroked his head and face with cool, soft hands, took the dressing from his leg, rubbed it with something that smelled like roses, and then waved her hands over him three times. At the last wave of her hands everything vanished, he felt himself sinking into the profoundest slumber, and remembered nothing more until he awoke in earnest.

The setting moon was throwing a feeble light through the casement, and the house was full of uproar. There was soft, heavy multitudinous stamping, a clashing and clanging of weapons, the voices of men and the cries of women, mixed with a hideous bellowing, which sounded victorious. The cobs were in the house! He sprang from his bed, hurried on some of his clothes, not forgetting his shoes, which were armed with nails; then spying an old hunting-knife, or short sword, hanging on the wall, he caught it, and rushed down the stairs, guided by the sounds of strife, which grew louder and louder.

When he reached the ground floor he found the whole place swarming. All the goblins of the mountain seemed gathered there. He rushed amongst them, shouting:

> One, two,
> Hit and hew!
> Three, four,
> Blast and bore!

and with every rhyme he came down a great stamp upon a foot, cutting at the same time their faces—executing, indeed, a sword dance of the wildest description. Away scattered the goblins in every direction—into closets, up stairs, into chimneys, up on rafters, and down to the cellars. Curdie went on stamping and slashing and singing, but saw nothing of the people of the house until he came to the great hall, in which, the moment he entered it, arose a great goblin shout. The last of the men-at-arms, the captain himself, was on the floor, buried beneath a wallowing crowd of goblins. For, while each knight was busy defending himself as well as he could, by stabs in the thick bodies of the goblins, for he had soon found their heads all but invulnerable, the queen had attacked his legs and feet with her horrible granite shoe, and he was soon down. But the captain had got his back to the wall and stood out longer. The goblins would have torn them all to pieces, but the king had given orders to carry them away alive, and over each of them, in twelve groups, was standing a knot of goblins, while as many as could find room were sitting upon their prostrate bodies.

Curdie burst in dancing and gyrating and stamping and singing like a small incarnate whirlwind.

> Where 'tis all a hole, sir,
> Never can be holes:
> Why should their shoes have soles, sir,
>   When they've got no souls?
>
> But she upon her foot, sir,
>   Has a granite shoe:

> *The strongest leather boot, sir,*
> *Six would soon be through.*

The queen gave a howl of rage and dismay, and before she recovered her presence of mind, Curdie, having begun with the group nearest him, had eleven of the knights on their legs again.

"Stamp on their feet!" he cried as each man rose, and in a few minutes the hall was nearly empty, the goblins running from it as fast as they could, howling and shrieking and limping, and cowering every now and then as they ran to cuddle their wounded feet in their hard hands, or to protect them from the frightful stamp-stamp of the armed men.

And now Curdie approached the group which, trusting in the queen and her shoe, kept their guard over the prostrate captain. The king sat on the captain's head, but the queen stood in front, like an infuriated cat, with her perpendicular eyes gleaming green, and her hair standing half up from her horrid head. Her heart was quaking, however, and she kept moving about her skin-shod foot with nervous apprehension. When Curdie was within a few paces, she rushed at him, made one tremendous stamp at his opposing foot, which happily he withdrew in time, and caught him round the waist, to dash him on the marble floor. But just as she caught him, he came down with all the weight of his iron-shod shoe upon her skin-shod foot, and with a hideous howl she dropped him, squatted on the floor, and took her foot in both her hands. Meanwhile the rest rushed on the king and the bodyguard, sent them flying, and lifted the prostrate captain, who was all but pressed to death. It was some moments before he recovered breath and consciousness.

"Where's the princess?" cried Curdie, again and again.

No one knew, and off they all rushed in search of her.

Through every room in the house they went, but nowhere was she to be found. Neither was one of the servants to be seen. But Curdie, who had kept to the lower part of the house, which was now quiet enough, began to hear a confused sound as of a distant hubbub, and set out to find where it came from. The noise grew as his sharp ears guided him to a stair and so to the wine cellar. It was full of goblins, whom the butler was supplying with wine as fast as he could draw it.

While the queen and her party had encountered the men-at-arms, Harelip with another company had gone off to search the house. They captured everyone they met, and when they could find no more, they hurried away to carry them safe to the caverns below. But when the butler, who was amongst them, found that their path lay through the wine cellar, he bethought himself of persuading them to taste the wine, and, as he had hoped, they no sooner tasted than they wanted more. The routed goblins, on their way below, joined them, and when Curdie entered they were all, with outstretched hands, in which were vessels of every description from saucepan to silver cup, pressing around the butler, who sat at the tap of a huge cask, filling and filling. Curdie cast one glance around the place before commencing his attack, and saw in the farthest corner a terrified group of the domestics unwatched, but cowering without courage to attempt their escape. Amongst them was the terror-stricken face of Lootie, but nowhere could he see the princess. Seized with the horrible conviction that Harelip had already carried her off, he rushed amongst them, unable for wrath to sing anymore, but stamping and cutting with greater fury than ever.

"Stamp on their feet, stamp on their feet!" he shouted, and in a moment the goblins were disappearing through the hole in the floor like rats and mice.

They could not vanish so fast, however, but that many more goblin feet had to go limping back over the underground ways of the mountain that morning.

Presently, however, they were reinforced from above by the king and his party, with the redoubtable queen at their head. Finding Curdie again busy amongst her unfortunate subjects, she rushed at him once more with the rage of despair, and this time gave him a bad bruise on the foot. Then a regular stamping fight got up between them, Curdie, with the point of his hunting knife, keeping her from clasping her mighty arms about him, as he watched his opportunity of getting once more a good stamp at her skin-shod foot. But the queen was more wary as well as more agile than hitherto.

The rest, meantime, finding their adversary thus matched for the moment, paused in their headlong hurry, and turned to the shivering group of women in the corner. As if determined to emulate his father and have a sun-woman of some sort to share his future throne, Harelip rushed at them, caught up Lootie, and sped with her to the hole. She gave a great shriek, and Curdie heard her, and saw the plight she was in. Gathering all his strength, he gave the queen a sudden cut across the face with his weapon, came down, as she started back, with all his weight on the proper foot, and sprang to Lootie's rescue. The prince had two defenseless feet, and on both of them Curdie stamped just as he reached the hole. He dropped his burden and rolled shrieking into the earth. Curdie made one stab at him as he disappeared, caught hold of the senseless Lootie, and having dragged her back to the corner, there mounted guard over her, preparing once more to encounter the queen. Her face streaming with blood, and her eyes flashing green lightning through it, she came on with her mouth open and her teeth grinning like a tiger's, followed by the king and her bodyguard of the thickest goblins. But the same moment in rushed the captain and his men, and ran at them stamping furiously. They dared not encounter such an onset. Away they scurried, the queen foremost. Of course, the right thing would have been to take the king and queen prisoners, and hold them hostages for the princess, but they were so anxious to find her that no one thought of detaining them until it was too late.

Having thus rescued the servants, they set about searching the house once more. None of them could give the least information concerning the princess. Lootie was almost silly with terror, and, although scarcely able to walk, would not leave Curdie's side for a single moment. Again he allowed the others to search the rest of the house—where, except a dismayed goblin lurking here and there, they found no one—while he requested Lootie to take him to the princess's room. She was as submissive and obedient as if he had been the king.

He found the bedclothes tossed about, and most of them on the floor, while the princess's garments were scattered all over the room, which was in the greatest confusion. It was only too evident that the goblins had been there, and Curdie had no longer any doubt that she had been carried off at the very first of the inroad. With a pang of despair he saw how wrong they had been in not securing the king and queen and prince, but he determined to find and rescue the princess as she had found and rescued him, or meet the worst fate to which the goblins could doom him.

Chapter 28

Curdie's Guide

*J*UST as the consolation of this resolve dawned upon his mind and he was turning away for the cellar to follow the goblins into their hole, something touched his hand. It was the slightest touch, and when he looked he could see nothing. Feeling and peering about in the gray of the dawn, his fingers came upon a tight thread. He looked again, and narrowly, but still could see nothing. It flashed upon him that this must be the princess's thread. Without saying a word, for he knew no one would believe him any more than he had believed the princess, he followed the thread with his finger, contrived to give Lootie the slip, and was soon out of the house and on the mountainside—surprised that, if the thread were indeed the grandmother's messenger, it should have led the princess, as he supposed it must, into the mountain, where she would be certain to meet the goblins rushing back enraged from their defeat. But he hurried on in the hope of overtaking her first. When he arrived, however, at the place where the path turned off for the mine, he found that the thread did not turn with it, but went straight up the mountain. Could it be that the thread was leading him home to his mother's cottage? Could the princess be there? He bounded up the mountain like one of its own goats, and before the sun was up, the thread had brought him indeed to his mother's door. There it vanished from his fingers, and he could not find it, search as he might.

The door was on the latch, and he entered. There sat his mother by the fire, and in her arms lay the princess fast asleep.

"Hush, Curdie!" said his mother. "Do not wake her. I'm so glad you're come! I thought the cobs must have got you again!"

With a heart full of delight, Curdie sat down at a corner of the hearth, on a stool opposite his mother's chair, and gazed at the princess, who slept as peacefully as if she had been in her own bed. All at once she opened her eyes and fixed them on him.

"Oh, Curdie! You're come!" she said quietly. "I thought you would!"

Curdie rose and stood before her with downcast eyes.

"Irene," he said, "I am very sorry I did not believe you."

"Oh, never mind, Curdie!" answered the princess. "You couldn't, you know. You do believe me now, don't you?"

"I can't help it now. I ought to have helped it before."

"Why can't you help it now?"

"Because, just as I was going into the mountain to look for you, I got hold of your thread, and it brought me here."

"Then you've come from my house, have you?"

"Yes, I have."

"I didn't know you were there."

"I've been there two or three days, I believe."

"And I never knew it! Then perhaps you can tell me why my grandmother has brought me here? I can't think. Something woke me—I didn't know what, but I was frightened, and I felt for the thread, and there it was! I was more frightened still when it brought me out on the mountain, for I thought it was going to take me into it again, and I like the outside of it best. I supposed you were in trouble again, and I had to get you out. But it brought me here instead, and, oh, Curdie, your mother has been so kind to me—just like my own grandmother!"

Here Curdie's mother gave the princess a hug, and the princess turned and gave her a sweet smile, and held up her mouth to kiss her.

"Then you didn't see the cobs?" asked Curdie.

"No. I haven't been into the mountain, I told you, Curdie."

"But the cobs have been into your house—all over it—and into your bedroom, making such a row!"

"What did they want there? It was very rude of them."

"They wanted you—to carry you off into the mountain with them, for a wife to their prince Harelip."

"Oh, how dreadful!" cried the princess, shuddering.

"But you needn't be afraid, you know. Your grandmother takes care of you."

"Ah! You do believe in my grandmother, then? I'm so glad! She made me think you would someday."

All at once Curdie remembered his dream, and was silent, thinking.

"But how did you come to be in my house, and me not know it?" asked the princess.

Then Curdie had to explain everything—how he had watched for her sake, how he had been wounded and shut up by the soldiers, how he heard the noises and could not rise, and how the beautiful old lady had come to him, and all that followed.

"Poor Curdie! To lie there hurt and ill, and me never to

know it!" exclaimed the princess, stroking his rough hand. "I would have come and nursed you, if they had told me."

"I didn't see you were lame," said his mother.

"Am I, Mother? Oh—yes—I suppose I ought to be. I declare I've never thought of it since I got up to go down amongst the cobs!"

"Let me see the wound," said his mother.

He pulled down his stocking—when behold, except a great scar, his leg was perfectly sound!

Curdie and his mother gazed in each other's eyes, full of wonder, but Irene called out: "I thought so, Curdie! I was sure it wasn't a dream. I was sure my grandmother had been to see you. Don't you smell the roses? It was my grandmother healed your leg, and sent you to help me."

"No, Princess Irene," said Curdie, "I wasn't good enough to be allowed to help you: I didn't believe you. Your grandmother took care of you without me."

"She sent you to help my people, anyhow. I wish my king-papa would come. I do want so to tell him how good you have been!"

"But," said the mother, "we are forgetting how frightened your people must be. You must take the princess home at once, Curdie—or at least go and tell them where she is."

"Yes, Mother. Only I'm dreadfully hungry. Do let me have some breakfast first. They ought to have listened to me, and then they wouldn't have been taken by surprise as they were."

"That is true, Curdie. But it is not for you to blame them much. You remember?"

"Yes, Mother, I do. Only I must really have something to eat."

"You shall, my boy—as fast as I can get it," said his mother, rising and setting the princess on her chair.

But before his breakfast was ready, Curdie jumped up so suddenly as to startle both his companions.

"Mother, Mother!" he cried, "I was forgetting. You must take the princess home yourself. I must go and wake my father."

Without a word of explanation, he rushed to the place where his father was sleeping. Having thoroughly roused him with what he told him, he darted out of the cottage.

Chapter 29

Masonwork

*H*E had all at once remembered the resolution of the goblins to carry out their second plan upon the failure of the first. No doubt they were already busy, and the mine was therefore in the greatest danger of being flooded and rendered useless—not to speak of the lives of the miners.

When he reached the mouth of the mine, after rousing all the miners within reach, he found his father and a good many more just entering. They all hurried to the gang by which he had found a way into the goblin country. There the foresight of Peter had already collected a great many blocks of stone, with cement, ready for building up the weak place—well enough known to the goblins. Although there was not room for more than two to be actually building at once, they managed, by setting all the rest to work in preparing the cement and passing the stones, to finish in the course of the day a huge buttress filling the whole gang, and supported everywhere by the live rock. Before the hour when they usually dropped work, they were satisfied the mine was secure.

They had heard goblin hammers and pickaxes busy all the time, and at length fancied they heard sounds of water they had never heard before. But that was otherwise accounted for when they left the mine, for they stepped out into a tremendous storm which was raging all over the mountain. The thunder was bellowing, and the lightning lancing out of a huge black cloud which lay above it and hung down its edges of thick mist over its sides. The lightning was breaking out of the mountain, too, and flashing up into the cloud. From the state of the brooks, now swollen into raging torrents, it was evident that the storm had been storming all day.

The wind was blowing as if it would blow him off the mountain, but, anxious about his mother and the princess, Curdie darted up through the thick of the tempest. Even if they had not set out before the storm came on, he did not judge them safe, for in such a storm even their poor little house was in danger. Indeed he soon found that but for a huge rock against which it was built, and which protected it from the blasts and the waters, it must have been swept if it was not blown away, for the two torrents into which this rock parted the rush of water behind it united again in front of the cottage— two roaring and dangerous streams, which his mother and the princess could not possibly have passed. It was with great difficulty that he forced his way through one of them, and up to the door.

The moment his hand fell on the latch, through all the uproar of winds and waters came the joyous cry of the princess: "There's Curdie! Curdie! Curdie!"

She was sitting wrapped in blankets on the bed, his mother trying for the hundredth time to light the fire which had been drowned by the rain that came down the chimney. The clay floor was one mass of mud, and the whole place looked wretched. But the faces of the mother and the princess shone as if their troubles only made them the merrier. Curdie burst out laughing at the sight of them.

"I never *had* such fun!" said the princess, her eyes twinkling and her pretty teeth shining. "How nice it must be to live in a cottage on the mountain!"

"It all depends on what kind your inside house is," said the mother.

"I know what you mean," said Irene. "That's the kind of thing my grandmother says."

By the time Peter returned the storm was nearly over, but the streams were so fierce and so swollen that it was not only out of the question for the princess to go down the mountain, but most dangerous for Peter even or Curdie to make the attempt in the gathering darkness.

"They will be dreadfully frightened about you," said Peter to the princess, "but we cannot help it. We must wait till the morning."

With Curdie's help, the fire was lighted at last, and the mother set about making their supper; and after supper they all told the princess stories till she grew sleepy. Then Curdie's mother laid her in Curdie's bed, which was in a tiny little garret room. As soon as she was in bed, through a little window low down in the roof she caught sight of her grandmother's lamp shining faraway beneath, and she gazed at the beautiful silvery globe until she fell asleep.

Chapter 30

The King and the Kiss

*T*HE next morning the sun rose so bright that Irene said the rain had washed his face and let the light out clean. The torrents were still roaring down the side of the mountain, but they were so much smaller as not to be dangerous in the daylight. After an early breakfast, Peter went to his work and Curdie and his mother set out to take the princess home. They had difficulty in getting her dry across the streams, and Curdie had again and again to carry her, but at last they got safe on the broader part of the road, and walked gently down toward the king's house. And what should they see as they turned the last corner but the last of the king's troop riding through the gate!

"Oh, Curdie!" cried Irene, clapping her hands right joyfully, "my king-papa is come."

The moment Curdie heard that, he caught her up in his arms and set off at full speed, crying, "Come on, Mother dear! The king may break his heart before he knows that she is safe."

Irene clung round his neck and he ran with her like a deer.

When he entered the gate into the court, there sat the king on his horse, with all the people of the house about him, weeping and hanging their heads. The king was not weeping, but his face was white as a dead man's, and he looked as if the life had gone out of him. The men-at-arms he had brought with him sat with horror-stricken faces, but eyes flashing with rage, waiting only for the word of the king to do something—they did not know what, and nobody knew what.

The day before, the men-at-arms belonging to the house, as soon as they were satisfied the princess had been carried away, rushed after the goblins into the hole, but found that they had already so skillfully blockaded the narrowest part, not many feet below the cellar, that without miners and their tools they could do nothing. Not one of them knew where the mouth of the mine lay, and some of those who had set out to find it had been overtaken by the storm and had not even yet returned. Poor Sir Walter was especially filled with shame, and almost hoped the king would order his head to be cut off, for to think of that sweet little face down amongst the goblins was unendurable.

When Curdie ran in at the gate with the princess in his arms, they were all so absorbed in their own misery and awed by the king's presence and grief, that no one observed his arrival. He went straight up to the king, where he sat on his horse.

"Papa! Papa!" the princess cried, stretching out her arms to him. "Here I am!"

The king started. The color rushed to his face. He gave an inarticulate cry. Curdie held up the princess, and the king bent down and took her from his arms. As he clasped her to his bosom, the big tears went dropping down his cheeks and his beard. And such a shout arose from all the bystanders that the startled horses pranced and capered, and the armor rang and clattered, and the rocks of the mountain echoed back the noises. The princess greeted them all as she nestled in her father's bosom, and the king did not set her down until she had told them all the story. But she had more to tell about Curdie than about herself, and what she did tell about herself none of them could understand except the king and Curdie, who stood by the king's knee stroking the neck of the great white horse. And still as she told what Curdie had done, Sir Walter and others added to what she told, even Lootie joining in the praises of his courage and energy.

Curdie held his peace, looking quietly up in the king's face. And his mother stood on the outskirts of the crowd listening with delight, for her son's deeds were pleasant in her ears, until the princess caught sight of her.

"And there is his mother, King-papa!" she said. "See—there. She is such a nice mother, and has been so kind to me!"

They all parted asunder as the king made a sign to her to come forward. She obeyed, and he gave her his hand, but could not speak.

"And now, King-papa," the princess went on, "I must tell you another thing. One night long ago Curdie drove the goblins away and brought Lootie and me safe from the mountain. And I promised him a kiss when we got home, but Lootie wouldn't let me give it him. I don't want you to scold Lootie, but I want you to tell her that a princess *must* do as she promises."

"Indeed she must, my child—except it be wrong," said the king. "There, give Curdie a kiss."

And as he spoke he held her toward him.

The princess reached down, threw her arms round Curdie's

neck and kissed him on the mouth, saying, "There, Curdie! There's the kiss I promised you!"

Then they all went into the house, and the cook rushed to the kitchen and the servants to their work. Lootie dressed Irene in her shiningest clothes, and the king put off his armor, and put on purple and gold; and a messenger was sent for Peter and all the miners, and there was a great and a grand feast, which continued long after the princess was put to bed.

Chapter 31

The Subterranean Waters

THE king's harper, who always formed a part of his escort, was chanting a ballad which he made as he went on playing on his instrument—about the princess and the goblins, and the prowess of Curdie, when all at once he ceased, with his eyes on one of the doors of the hall. Thereupon the eyes of the king and his guests turned thitherward also. The next moment, through the open doorway came the Princess Irene. She went straight up to her father, with her right hand stretched out a little sideways, and her forefinger, as her father and Curdie understood, feeling its way along the invisible thread. The king took her on his knee, and she said in his ear, "King-papa, do you hear that noise?"

"I hear nothing," said the king.

"Listen," she said, holding up her forefinger.

The king listened, and a great stillness fell upon the company. Each man, seeing that the king listened, listened also, and the harper sat with his harp between his arms, and his fingers silent upon the strings.

"I do hear a noise," said the king at length, "a noise as of distant thunder. It is coming nearer and nearer. What can it be?"

They all heard it now, and each seemed ready to start to his feet as he listened. Yet all sat perfectly still. The noise came rapidly nearer.

"What *can* it be?" said the king again.

"I think it must be another storm coming over the mountain," said Sir Walter.

Then Curdie, who at the first word of the king had slipped from his seat, and laid his ear to the ground, rose up quickly, and approaching the king said, speaking very fast, "Please, Your Majesty, I think I know what it is. I have no time to explain, for that might make it too late for some of us. Will Your Majesty give orders that everybody leave the house as quickly as possible and get up the mountain?"

The king, who was the wisest man in the kingdom, knew well there was a time when things must be done and questions left till afterward. He had faith in Curdie, and rose instantly, with Irene in his arms.

"Every man and woman follow me," he said, and strode out into the darkness.

Before he had reached the gate, the noise had grown to a great thundering roar, and the ground trembled beneath their feet, and before the last of them had crossed the court, out after them from the great hall door came a huge rush of turbid water, and almost swept them away. But they got safe out of the gate and up the mountain, while the torrent went roaring down the road into the valley beneath.

Curdie had left the king and the princess to look after his

mother, whom he and his father, one on each side, caught up when the stream overtook them and carried safe and dry.

When the king had got out of the way of the water, a little up the mountain, he stood with the princess in his arms, looking back with amazement on the issuing torrent, which glimmered fierce and foamy through the night. There Curdie rejoined them.

"Now, Curdie," said the king, "what does it mean? Is this what you expected?"

"It is, Your Majesty," said Curdie, and proceeded to tell him about the second scheme of the goblins, who, fancying the miners of more importance to the upper world than they were, had resolved, if they should fail in carrying off the king's daughter, to flood the mine and drown the miners. Then he explained what the miners had done to prevent it. The goblins had, in pursuance of their design, let loose all the underground reservoirs and streams, expecting the water to run down into the mine, which was lower than their part of the mountain, for they had, as they supposed, not knowing of the solid wall close behind, broken a passage through into it. But the readiest outlet the water could find had turned out to be the tunnel they had made to the king's house, the possibility of which catastrophe had not occurred to the young miner until he had laid his ear to the floor of the hall.

What was then to be done? The house appeared in danger of falling, and every moment the torrent was increasing.

"We must set out at once," said the king. "But how to get at the horses!"

"Shall I see if we can manage that?" said Curdie.

"Do," said the king.

Curdie gathered the men-at-arms, and took them over the

garden wall, and so to the stables. They found their horses in
terror; the water was rising fast around them, and it was quite
time they were got out. But there was no way to get them out,
except by riding them through the stream, which was now
pouring from the lower windows as well as the door. As one
horse was quite enough for any man to manage through such a
torrent, Curdie got on the king's white charger and, leading the
way, brought them all in safety to the rising ground.

"Look, look, Curdie!" cried Irene, the moment that, having
dismounted, he led the horse up to the king.

Curdie did look, and saw, high in the air, somewhere about
the top of the king's house, a great globe of light, shining like
the purest silver.

"Oh!" he cried in some consternation, "that is your grandmother's lamp! We *must* get her out. I will go and find her. The
house may fall, you know."

"My grandmother is in no danger," said Irene, smiling.

"Here, Curdie, take the princess while I get on my horse,"
said the king.

Curdie took the princess again, and both turned their eyes to
the globe of light. The same moment there shot from it a white
bird, which, descending with outstretched wings, made one
circle round the king and Curdie and the princess, and then
glided up again. The light and the pigeon vanished together.

"Now, Curdie," said the princess as he lifted her to her
father's arms, "you see my grandmother knows all about it, and
isn't frightened. I believe she could walk through that water
and it wouldn't wet her a bit."

"But, my child," said the king, "you will be cold if you
haven't something more on. Run, Curdie, my boy, and fetch

anything you can lay your hands on, to keep the princess warm. We have a long ride before us."

Curdie was gone in a moment, and soon returned with a great rich fur, and the news that dead goblins were tossing about in the current through the house. They had been caught in their own snare. Instead of the mine they had flooded their own country, whence they were now swept up drowned. Irene shuddered, but the king held her close to his bosom. Then he turned to Sir Walter, and said, "Bring Curdie's father and mother here."

"I wish," said the king, when they stood before him. "to take your son with me. He shall enter my bodyguard at once, and wait further promotion."

Peter and his wife, overcome, only murmured almost inaudible thanks. But Curdie spoke aloud.

"Please, Your Majesty," he said, "I cannot leave my father and mother."

"That's right, Curdie!" cried the princess. "*I* wouldn't if I was you."

The king looked at the princess and then at Curdie with a glow of satisfaction on his countenance.

"I too think you are right, Curdie," he said, "and I will not ask you again. But I shall have a chance of doing something for you sometime."

"Your Majesty has already allowed me to serve you," said Curdie.

"But Curdie," said his mother, "why shouldn't you go with the king? We can get on very well without you."

"But I can't get on very well without you," said Curdie. "The king is very kind, but I could not be half the use to him that I am to you. Please, Your Majesty, if you wouldn't mind giving my mother a red petticoat! I should have got her one long ago, but for the goblins."

"As soon as we get home," said the king, "Irene and I will search out the warmest one to be found, and send it by one of the gentlemen."

"Yes, that we will, Curdie!" said the princess. "And next summer we'll come back and see you wear it, Curdie's mother," she added. "Shan't we, King-papa?"

"Yes, my love, I hope so," said the king.

Then, turning to the miners, he said, "Will you do the best you can for my servants tonight? I hope they will be able to return to the house tomorrow."

The miners with one voice promised their hospitality.

Then the king commanded his servants to mind whatever Curdie should say to them, and after shaking hands with him and his father and mother, the king and the princess and all their company rode away down the side of the new stream, which had already devoured half the road, into the starry night.

Chapter 32

The Last Chapter

*A*LL the rest went up the mountain, and separated in groups to the homes of the miners. Curdie and his father and mother took Lootie with them. And the whole way a light, of which all but Lootie understood the origin, shone upon their path. But when they looked round they could see nothing of the silvery globe.

For days and days the water continued to rush from the doors and windows of the king's house, and a few goblin bodies were swept out into the road.

Curdie saw that something must be done. He spoke to his father and the rest of the miners, and they at once proceeded to make another outlet for the waters. By setting all hands to the work, tunneling here and building there, they soon succeeded, and having also made a little tunnel to drain the water away from the king's house, they were soon able to get into the wine cellar, where they found a multitude of dead goblins—among the rest the queen, with the skin-shoe gone, and the stone one fast to her ankle—for the water had swept away the barricade which prevented the men-at-arms from following the goblins, and had greatly widened the passage. They built it securely up, and then went back to their labors in the mine.

A good many of the goblins with their creatures escaped from the inundation out upon the mountain. But most of them soon left that part of the country, and most of those who remained grew milder in character, and indeed became very much like the Scotch Brownies. Their skulls became softer as well as their hearts, and their feet grew harder, and by degrees they became friendly with the inhabitants of the mountain and even with the miners. But the latter were merciless to any of the cobs' creatures that came in their way, until at length they all but disappeared.

The rest of the history of *The Princess and Curdie* must be kept for another volume.

Afterword

Andre Norton

*A*t a very much younger age I came to *The Princess and the Goblin* by the back door, as one might say. Its sequel (*The Princess and Curdie*) was given to me as a birthday present when I was about ten or so, before I knew that there was another book about the mountain-haunting goblins, Princess Irene, and the sturdy, dependable Curdie. My birthday book was devoured in one gulp and then I searched library shelves for more books by the same author. Having so discovered *The Princess and the Goblin*, I was entranced to see how the story really began. For some time the thought of the goblin queen's fearsome stone shoes remained with me—certainly a new and unusual weapon to be used against dark forces, perfect to wear clumping about in the night of underground.

Some of MacDonald's work seems by our standards today to be turgid and oversentimental, lacking any spell for readers who have had dealings with Tolkien's orcs and the like. His style is consciously that of a storyteller instead of a writer, and his moralizing becomes heavy-handed.

But once he forgets he is writing for "dear little children" lapped about by the snug safety of a Victorian nursery or schoolroom, he spins an exciting tale. He explores some points that are of prime importance today—namely, the wrong in dismissing as nonexistent that which cannot be understood. The frustration of those telling the truth after encountering some wonder and not being believed, or being declared a liar, can still strike a spark from a reader.

One who has read of the mores of the Victorian period can agree that such frustration must have been common to children. By custom they lived so far apart from most adults in even middle-class families that they did indeed have little common ground with those of an older generation. One was taught then to accept all that was said by an adult without asking any questions. Quick punishment for "naughtiness" was the result of asking why.

Our modern robust fantasy does not contain this gulf between generations. But MacDonald's picture of a grandmother (fairy, of course) who is visible only when she is believed in was a telling argument for faith in his day and age.

Belief without physical proof, openness of mind to the wonders of life about one, is the center theme of his books. And that is as important now as when they first appeared, in spite of what we would consider today quaint, "old-fashioned" style.

Though the goblins and their unfortunate animals will cause few shivers for those knowing orcs and the modern evil servants of the Dark, they still carry the taint of ugly wrongness. Only the goblin queen is given true menace. One is led to suspect that she may, consciously or unconsciously, be based on some overaggressive female (for that age) known to MacDonald. She is always represented in a temper, pushing the reluctant male members of her family into action. Of all the underground crew she is the most noxious.

As for the others, hunted out of their homes by the increasing demands of the miners, well, one wonders whether they did not indeed have rights worth fighting for. We must agree that their end of the tale is more fitting than a ruthless suppression of all their kind.

Just as the goblin queen is all-powerful underground, so is the elusive grandmother her balance above. A powerful godmother or grandmother is so usual a character in many fairy tales that it takes MacDonald's skill to make a notable success of Irene's great-great-relative. Her character is a major one (she shows even greater powers in *The Princess and Curdie*). One can close one's eyes and see her spinning magic, just as one can hear the far-off hum of her wheel.

George MacDonald wrote a number of fantasies—for both children and adults. *The Golden Key*, for example, is a small masterpiece, keeping within the limits of a novelette a complete allegory of life and death. Just as the Princess Irene, on a similar quest, must follow the invisible thread of faith through a dark she dreads in order to fulfill what she conceives to be her duty.

The power evoked in giving one's word is the second theme MacDonald stresses. We have gotten well away (we are smugly told) from stories that are occupied with openly stressed moral lessons. But old-fashioned values do carry weight. They certainly do with Princess Irene and Curdie, they even do with the goblins. A visible scale of justice waits to swing to the proper balance.

This book is exactly what developed when an adult with imagination, talent, and purpose said—"I'll tell you a story." The author meant to provide more than entertainment, he wished to underline right and wrong. That the story rises above the stressed conscientious moral purposes demanded in his day is due to MacDonald's own native genius. He is more than just offering a book to while away such a rainy day as sent Princess Irene exploring up a crooked hidden stair.

We live in a different age and by other standards, yet there is something strongly appealing in these firmly stated older codes of conduct. Sometimes black and white with no grays can be refreshingly secure.